CADE

JASPER SPRINGS

BOOK ONE

BY EVIE RILEY

Cade

An MM Opposites Attract Romance

Jasper Springs

Book One

Copyright © 2024

Evie Riley

Second Edition

ISBN: 978-1-77357-684-8

Published by Naughty Nights Press LLC

Cover Art By Willsin Rowe

CADE

Home is where the heart is...

Life in Jasper Springs may look perfect, but for Cade Green there's one thing still missing... a hunky billionaire to whisk him away, just like in the movies he can't stop binge watching after his latest break up. But life isn't some romantic tale for guys like him. That is, until the man of his dreams shows up at the local bar's karaoke night.

Can Cade's small-town heart handle the whirlwind that Weston brings?

Famed bachelor Weston Rhodes reluctantly returns to his hometown, planning on nothing more than a fleeting visit. The last thing he expects to find is a reason to stay. However, after one intense night, he soon discovers himself falling for the small town's adorable veterinarian.

Can Weston, used to city lights and endless possibilities, embrace a fairy-tale romance in his quaint hometown?

Readers seeking a small town good boy/bad boy billionaire, opposites attract romance set in a cozy little town may find this story hits those buttons.

While Cade and Weston may have cameos in future stories, each book in this series can be read as a standalone.

CHAPTER ONE

Cade

THE DRIVE THROUGH Jasper Springs was always the prettiest early in the morning. The sunrise colored the skies in various rich tones, from blush to ochre to lavender like some picturesque postcard, which was one of the things I had always loved about this town.

It was always warm, a comfortable seventy degrees even in the winter, which wasn't a terrible thing. I could have only imagined driving in snow, sleet and ice when there was an emergency at the Jasper Springs Pet Hospital, beholden to snow plow trucks and whatnot. In truth, I wasn't made for the cold, clearly.

EVIE RILEY

I drove past Jasper Springs High and turned up the radio. My heart ached at hearing the familiar melodic tones of Ariana Grande, if only because it reminded me of *him.* My ex.

I knew then in my heart we weren't meant to be. Hell, I knew when I started dating Bill, we were probably going to go up in flames, so I absolutely knew that I shouldn't have been so worked up over everything, but I thought... I thought maybe, just possibly I'd be proven wrong. And when we had passed that six-month mark, I thought maybe I was right. Maybe this one was different. But it turned out Bill was, in fact, not much different from any of my former flames.

The "it's not you, it's me" shit? Yeah, I'm a magnet for that.

Most of the men I met were fun for a little while, but eventually my "small town charm" became less refreshing, and more of a thorn in everyone's sides.

Just because I don't see myself leaving Jasper Springs any time doesn't mean I don't have value, or that I'm not willing to make something long-distance work.

Ariana's voice on the radio droned on about letting go.

But life wasn't a Hallmark movie, either. There weren't exactly many big city boys coming to tiny little Jasper Springs looking for a small town guy wearing flannel to sweep them off their feet.

A man can dream, right?

Just as I pulled into my usual parking space in front of the pet hospital, my phone went off, that annoying siren ringtone somehow knowing just the exact moment to pull me from my thoughts.

Out of all the men I'd loved before, Dawson was the only one I could actually wholeheartedly agree that we made better friends than we ever did as lovers.

Granted the sex wasn't half bad, but we're both way too different for things to have ever worked on a non-platonic level.

As it was our relationship didn't last long before we both realized that we just didn't feel the way we probably should have.

It was the most mutual "it's not you, it's me" I'd ever been in, because for once I actually delivered the speech, and Dawson just shrugged, as if it didn't matter. And then he asked me if I wanted pepperoni on the pizza.

And of course, I had agreed.

Is there anything better than a pepperoni pizza?

It's classic.

Punching the green icon and silencing the trill, I sighed upon answering, knowing if I didn't, Dawson would just keep calling until I would inevitably lose my shit, despite the fact he knew I was working.

"Yes, Dawson?" I deadpanned.

The man is natural cocaine, I swear to God. His energy can be felt before he even speaks.

"M's Place put up their Bar Bingo & Karaoke schedule today," Dawson said with absolute delight as I let out a sigh.

It never bothered me, living in a small town, but there wasn't much to do around Jasper Springs other than hang out at M's Place or one of the coffee shops or few restaurants that exist. Of course there was a movie theater, a gym, a baseball field...

But entertainment was still pretty minimal. Most of the folks from Jasper Springs liked it that way, but for the social butterflies like Dawson, there was always M's Place.

Our friend Mitchell's brother, Miguel,

owned the bar, and while they were most definitely classified as a "dive bar", they hosted a good amount of events. Everything from holiday parties to trivia nights, to Bar Bingo and karaoke.

And they're not douchebags when it comes to being openly queer either, being as Mitchell is about as openly gay as one can get.

I pursed my lips. I wished I could have the confidence that Mitchell and Dawson had when it came to social situations like that, but I was about as social as a clam at a clambake.

"And?" I huffed.

"And, it's *tonight.* You work until four, right?" Dawson pressed.

I knew exactly what he was getting at, and I also knew I should say no. That I should just put in my hours, go home, eat some ice cream and call it a night.

But I hadn't seen Mitch or Dawson since Bill and I broke up right before Christmas…

Who breaks up right before Christmas?

Worst holiday movie ever…

"I do, but that doesn't mean—"

"What? Like you have something better to do? Stay home in your fluffy bunny slippers eating your weight in Rocky Road?" Dawson drawled sarcastically.

I was both aggravated at the fact that the firefighter knew me so well, and offended that Dawson didn't think that was precisely my idea of a good time.

I just wish I didn't have to do it alone.

"Way to be harsh, Dawson."

"I'm sorry, man, but it's for your own good. You're just nursing the wound at this point. Time to take off the band-aid. Get back out there. Catch some bigger fish to make you forget all about Billiard-No-Brains," Dawson encouraged.

I rolled my eyes at my friend's nickname for my most recent ex.

Dawson had given him the nickname when Bill lost a game of pool to him and Mitch. Ultimately, it was a shitty call. Bill shot for a higher ball, when he clearly could have had an easy point, and it cost us the game. Dawson had taken it upon himself to refer to him as nothing else since, except, of course, in his actual presence. Though I did always worry that he was going to slip up eventually.

Guess I don't have to worry about that anymore.

I rolled my eyes again at Dawson's

tone, running my hand over my face and let out a deep sigh.

I knew without a doubt that I wouldn't say no, because whether I liked it or not, Dawson was right.

I need to get out, to get myself back on track and put Billiard-No-Brains behind me.

"Yeah, okay." I conceded. "I got to go, Diane is probably wondering why I'm still sitting in the car," I said quickly.

"Excellent!" Dawson said, his tone something between a cartoon villain and a man who just won the lottery. I hung up, breathing a sigh of defeat.

It was just an evening out with friends, catching up.

What was the worst that could happen?

CHAPTER TWO

Cade

THE BAR WAS packed, as was typical for Bar Bingo & karaoke. Jasper Springs wasn't exactly the biggest town on the map by far, but it wasn't uncommon for some of the folks from the neighboring towns of Paradise and Deer Hills to mosey on over to M's for the Bar Bingo nights.

Dawson slammed down his beer, rolling his eyes.

"Come on, Cade. Live a little, have some fun for once," he taunted me.

Dawson had been trying to get me up on stage to karaoke for the last hour, despite the fact he knew how much I despised that kind of thing.

It's not that I couldn't sing, because I very well could. I just didn't normally do that sort of thing outside of my house or car, and I wasn't the type to seek out attention. Everyone's eyes on me would make me nervous, but Dawson told me no one would be paying any real attention to me.

I'm not sure if that made it better or worse, to be honest.

"Leave the boy alone, Dawson," Mitchell said, taking pity on me as usual. I'd known Mitch since the sixth grade, though I'd never really considered him a best friend or anything, but nowadays I felt differently. Though I knew many people, I was closest to Dawson and Mitch, and did consider them my best friends.

They have definitely been the most consistent men in my life.

"Ya'll are lame. I'm going up," Dawson said as he left us at the high-top table.

My gaze danced around the room, taking in the sight of plenty of the other men, and even the women who all seemed like they were having a blast. A part of me wondered if I'd ever feel that vibrant again. Like I was on top of the world. Because as I watched them all, I couldn't help but feel forever stuck in the bottom of the world.

As I people watched, I noticed a man I had certainly never seen before. While I'd never been the biggest social butterfly, I did know a good bit of folks from Paradise and Deer Hills, if only through treating their pets. A natural observer, I knew without a doubt that I had never seen this guy before.

For starters, he looked a little too... nice to be in M's Place. A perfectly tailored, rather expensive looking suit like his would stick out in any bar whose idea of fancy is putting a tiny umbrella in the frozen drinks.

I started at the man's feet, noticing the perfectly shined leather shoes that looked like they cost more than my car. My eyes widened as my gaze traveled up slender legs that looked like they went on for miles by the posture of how he straddled his bar stool. I watched intently as the attractive stranger pushed back the bottom of his suit jacket, his long, lithe fingers sliding along the top of his thigh. Instantly, I found myself imagining what that would feel like, those fingers brushing *my thighs*. I blushed from the immediate thoughts, but couldn't turn away. When my roving gaze finally made it to the man's face, I thought maybe I *had* imagined him completely.

Maybe the two beers I'd had were getting to me.

Because I swore this man looked like someone straight out of a Hallmark movie.

What were the chances he was gay?

Probably slim, but I could dream, right?

No rules against fantasizing...

Instantly, my cock twitched as I watched him shift his stance. The way this man held himself, so sure, and confident.

Not to mention that sexy smile.

I knew he was out of my league.

If he's even batting for the same team, that is.

His demeanor alone screamed "rich asshole", which should have deterred me, but only made me want him that much more because that's how fucked up *I* was.

Why am I always attracted to assholes?

CADE

What is my problem?

I chastised myself as I fought the urge to stare.

Assholes will always treat you like shit, Cade. You need a gentleman. Someone like you.

My mother's words echoed in my head. I couldn't blame the woman for trying to impart some sense in me, but I didn't think she understood that the selection pool for me wasn't exactly full of the men she read about in her romance books.

That's when I saw that Hottie-McSuit was staring back at *me* with a smirk.

Right at me.

His dark eyes sparkled with a fire that called to my twitching cock, and I knew I should look away, but I was powerless to do so.

Nope, I was truly frozen in this man's gaze, my skin feeling suddenly flushed as his delicious lips curved into a smile and he winked at me.

Oh fuck.

Fuck fuck, fuckity fuck.

Well, that cleared some things up, I supposed. But he was still out of my league. He was probably out of my ballpark entirely.

I could hear the end of Dawson's song, Nickelback's Photograph, just as the man from my absolute dreams climbed off his barstool, sliding his hands in his suit jacket pockets. He sauntered toward me, his gaze never breaking, and I felt the world around me still.

Why did we have to pick a table in the center of the room, damn it?

CHAPTER THREE

Weston

I LOATHED COMING home to Jasper Springs. I'd never really felt like I fit in, in the quaint, charming little town. Part of that surely had to do with the fact that I'd never spent more than the summer there, despite it being the town my family's business had been a part of for practically my entire life.

But being as my mother insisted on sending me to the highest accredited private schools my father's money could buy, that probably had a lot to do with such things, and my father only saw it as a means to an end.

Because to him, one day I'd take his

place as CEO of Rhodes Enterprises, whether I wanted to or not. This company, this legacy, belonged to me.

Not to mention all the money that came with it...

But to me, the town of Jasper Springs was just so... idyllic. Like something out of a damn rom-com movie.

The only thing to really do in the town was go to the damn bar. Nightlife was non-existent in Jasper Springs, and I'm pretty sure the closest club was at least an hour away in the city. At least the bartender could make a good Manhattan.

I was about to throw in the towel and ask for the check, because quite frankly, if I had to listen to the asshole on stage screeching along to Nickelback a second longer, I would have gone insane. I noticed the man across from the bar, the one who was sitting with Nickelback's rejected soloist, was staring at me.

I was used to being stared at, quite honestly. At the risk of sounding like an ass, I knew I was in fact, the best of both worlds when it came to my inherited good looks. My mother's pedigree was very visible in my bone structure and my dark green eyes, while I got all of my father's swagger and his full, thick chestnut hair.

Though the way this California-surfer cutie was looking at me went far beyond appreciation. His pretty little blue peepers stared at me with *hunger* and longing, and I couldn't help but smile.

Perhaps a good roll in the hay was just what I needed to get through this god-forsaken trip.

Hometown Heartthrob was actually pretty cute, if I was being honest.

I trailed my gaze over his form. I could tell by the polo shirt he was wearing, which looked a little tight around his arms, that Pretty-Blue-Eyes took good care of himself, went to the gym at least. But the way he sat on his barstool, how he hunched over just a bit, and blushed when he realized I had caught him looking, told me that he wasn't overly confident in himself.

I've always loved a good, shy boy. They're usually the dirtiest bastards in bed.

The screeching man finally finished his song, and not a moment too soon, breaking the adorable target out of his daze. I did make it a point to slowly saunter over in his direction, deciding on the way exactly which song I would select to make the damn fool drop to his knees.

Then I'd buy him a drink, and take him back to my hotel so he could really drop to his knees and suck my cock like a good, dirty boy.

As I walked past him, I made a point to get as close as possible, shooting him my telltale look that I was well aware made men like him weak.

The look that told them without a single word that they were mine for the night and they'd do as I asked.

It wasn't like anyone usually lasted longer than that anyway, and by the time the sun came up, I would be off somewhere new. Long-term relationships didn't typically work for me.

My father liked to remind me that he was the same until he and my mom had set up shop in Jasper Springs. Until he'd met my mother, he had also been content with 'being a bachelor' as he called it. But after moving to Jasper Springs, and meeting my mom, they'd both settled down here after my mother got pregnant with me. Some people hated the constant traveling and jet-set life, like her. But business called for more jet setting after I was born, and the city was more manageable when we traveled so much.

Though I never hated it, in fact, it had been the only constant in my life. I didn't know how to stay in one place, because I'd never had to and there was a sort of poetry to that. New experiences, new men, new ways for me to pretend I was someone else...

But I'd be lying if I said I didn't think about the contrast sometimes.

Putting down roots, waking up to the same man every day, pushing a cart at the nearest Whole Foods while I drink my wheatgrass shake.

But was that really who Weston Rhodes was beneath the veneer of expensive suits and top notch clubs?

I shoved the thought aside as I grabbed the microphone from the DJ, whispering my song choice in his ear. I didn't see the point in shouting in the loud, god-forsaken place.

My father always told me you didn't need to be loud to make people listen. Whispering forced them to listen to you, they couldn't be distracted that way or some shit.

The intro beats filled the space and the

stage lights were bright, but I didn't blink. Instead, I only focused on finding Pretty-Blue-Eyes where he sat, and gave the best karaoke performance of my damn life.

Of course, I wouldn't have settled for anything less, and neither should he.

Something happened as the song droned on, as our eyes fell on one another. I knew halfway through as I watched his chest rise and fall, as I watched that hunger in the man's eyes turn into a starving need, that I had him.

I always got what I wanted, and that night I wanted him.

I graciously handed back the microphone to the DJ, and took my sweet old time approaching the object of my current desire.

"You were amazing up there," the other man said hurriedly as I leaned my hand on the table, steadying myself and standing in front of him like the piece of meat I knew that I was.

Grade A, baby.

"I know. I also know it'd be *amazing* if you let me buy you a drink. You look quite thirsty.," I said, flashing him a grin.

One of the other men at the table rolled his eyes, while the one that was screeching along before on stage just shoved Pretty-Blue-Eyes in front of me.

"Annnd this is where you say 'yes sir'," the screeching man said with a laugh.

I wasn't sure if he was taunting the object of my flirtation, or giving him a push of encouragement, but either way, something shifted in the man's gaze and he nodded quickly.

"Um, yeah... I mean, yes... I mean... sure. A drink sounds great," he said and I knew I had him. Hook, line, and sinker.

Yeah, I was definitely getting my dick sucked after this.

This trip was looking better already.

CHAPTER FOUR

Cade

IT'S JUST A drink, Cade. Not like you've never done this before or anything...

Though, I had to admit, something about Smooth-Suit-McGee buying me a drink felt drastically different from any other "let me buy you a drink's" I'd experienced.

If it wasn't for Dawson nearly shoving me off my damn barstool, I would have probably been a staring, speechless mess at the mountain of sex that stood in front of me. Up close, I could smell his rich, heady cologne and appreciate the finer details of his GQ-Model face. He was literally the hottest man I'd ever laid eyes on.

So I followed the man of my dreams to the bar like a moth to a flame, making our way through the crowd. When we finally got up to the bar, the patrons split like the Red Sea for us.

Well, him, technically. I'd always been about as invisible as they come, but for the moment I was riding the coattails of stardust, more than happy to bask in his starry glow.

God, he's really fucking gorgeous.

"What'll it be, darling?" he drawled as he leaned his long arms on the counter, the fabric of his jacket pulling at all the right places to showcase his form. He propped his foot up on the silver bar at the base, elongating the silhouette of his legs, and I couldn't help but get a good glance at his firm, tight ass.

I'm so out of my league.

"Well, usually I'm a Sam Adams guy," I said, trying to keep the shakiness out of my voice.

He nodded in response as he called Max, Miguel and Mitchell's sister, over. While the bar may have belonged to Miguel, it truly was a family affair. Max had been serving cocktails since the place opened, and the woman could make a mean Manhattan.

"Noted. Do you have a name or should I just call you Sam on account of your taste in beer?" He smirked, accompanied by a quick wink.

I couldn't help but shake my head at his sarcasm. Even his words were smooth, despite the fact they were sarcastic as hell.

I knew I should have been put off by his attitude, the fancy suit and the looks he kept throwing my way as he licked his lips, but damn it if I'm not an absolute sucker for an asshole.

If all you ever want is an asshole Cade, don't be surprised when they act like an asshole.

I sighed, looking up at the man in question, mesmerized by the pure fire in his dark green eyes.

I hate that I'm like this.

Why can't I just lust after normal, nice guys?

"It's Cade," I answered, as Max finally reached us and my dreamboat mystery man barked out an order of one Sam Adams and one glass of Oban on the rocks.

Max shot me a look I could only describe as judgmental, much like the one an older sister would give when you bring home the captain of the Lacrosse team for "study time."

Give me a break, Max!

Like you wouldn't accept a drink from a guy like...

Shit, I didn't even know his name. Either the alcohol was already getting to me, or Dawson was right, and I'd been cooped up too long mourning a breakup to the point I'd forgotten how to people.

"Should I call you *Oban-Wan Kenobi* or..." I regretted the words the minute they were out of my mouth, realizing how utterly stupid they sounded in reality. I'd always been terrible when it came to pick up lines. I thanked the stars every day for the invention of the dating app.

Truly, this shit is for the birds.

Max slid me my beer, shaking her head.

A little support would be nice, Max.

"I regret to inform you, young Padawan, I am not the Ewan McGregor you seek. Unfortunately," Hottie McSuit said with a sly grin.

"Although I can destroy that precious

mouth of yours like the Phantom Menace...” He winked at me, those delicious lips curving into a delectable smile, and my insides heated at the very sight.

Max rolled her eyes as she slid him his drink.

I knew then I should walk away. Take my drink, say thanks, and get the hell away from this selfish, sexy pile of sin who was causing my damn cock to twitch.

But I just didn’t know how to say no to pretty assholes like him.

Just as I opened my mouth to speak, the man took a sip of his drink, appraising me with an endearing gaze.

“It’s Weston.”

“Well, *Weston*, I appreciate the drink,” I said, flashing him with a cheeky grin of my own as I watched him take a sip of his drink.

“Well, perhaps you can pay me back?” he said with a raised eyebrow and I half thought he was going to ask me right then and there if I’d like to go home with him, and not even bother with pleasantries.

Weston didn’t exactly seem like the type to beat around the bush, and I knew even though I shouldn’t I’d probably say yes. After all, I knew Weston wasn't from around Jasper Springs, and maybe a dreamy, once in a lifetime fuck was just what I needed to move on from Billiard-No-Brains and get back to being a functional, stable adult.

Instead of the isolated, Netflix-binging, ice cream-eating hermit I've become. That's how it always works in the movies, anyway.

"Oh yeah, and how exactly do you expect me to... pay you back..." I nearly choked, thanks to swallowing a little too much beer.

I'm freaking hopeless...

Weston had the audacity to look at me like a little orphaned puppy as he drained his drink, pointing to the stage.

"Sing with me."

"You've got to be kidding me," I said, feeling a sense of panic. Karaoke really wasn't my thing, but something about the way Weston looked at me, his dark green eyes full of mischief, I felt... tempted. Comfortable, even.

"I'll make it easy. You can even pick the song," Weston said as he ran a hand over his shirt, smoothing out the miniscule wrinkles that probably only he could see.

Either that or he's just trying to get me to look at his chest, at the buttons he'd popped.

Which I'm powerless to resist...

"I'm not a very good singer," I said as I watched him set down his beer.

"Who said anything about being good? This isn't American Idol. I just want us to have some... fun."

The way Weston's voice hung on that last word, *fun...* made my insides turn to lava. And when he flashed his dark eyes at me, that look of mischief called to my soul in a way I'd never felt before.

It was just one song, what was the worst that could happen?

Right?

CHAPTER FIVE

Cade

I'D LOST TRACK of how many songs Weston and I had sung that night. How many songs *Weston* had sung...

I giggled as the beginning riffs of *Don't Go Breaking My Heart* filled the speakers, as Weston rolled up his sleeves, shaking his head.

At some point in the night—a point that I couldn't place to save my life—Weston had lost his suit jacket. His shirtsleeves were rolled up to the elbow to showcase his tanned, toned arms, and he'd popped more than a few buttons on his button up shirt. Under the lights of the stage, sweat gleamed off his exposed skin, and I felt *fantastic.* Better than I had in a long time.

Weston shook his hips as he brought the microphone to his lips, doing his best Elton John impression while I waited for my turn. He was hot as hell up there too, and I was fairly certain we were both sweating through our shirts, but I didn't care.

For the first time in what felt like forever, I didn't *care.* I was having a blast, and I didn't want it to end.

Like I knew it was going to.

"Don't go breaking my heart..." Weston sang, his perfectly pearly white smile making me feel even hotter under the damn lights.

"I won't go breaking your heart!" I sang in return as I pointed to Weston, but I only half sang-half laughed, because I couldn't control myself anymore, either.

I'd lost count of how many beers I'd knocked back with Weston, Dawson, and even Mitchell.

I haven't felt this good since before I met Bill...

Dawson burst out laughing as he threw on his jacket. The place was starting to clear out finally, and Max already announced last call.

Weston sauntered his way over to me, throwing one sweat-slicked arm around my shoulders as he pulled me close. The heat between us was damn near hellish from the lights and our combined sweat, and I leaned my head back against his warm shoulder as I wailed out the last bits of the song.

Weston's dark eyes sparkled with mischief, and up close like that I thought they kind of looked like semi-precious stones. My insides twisted and melted, and he smiled. A light chuckle made his chest vibrate against me. Through my hazy vision, I thought I could get lost there, staring at Weston, at his jeweled irises and perfect face.

Almost as if Weston could somehow sense my absolute mind meltdown, he whispered, "It's your turn."

I could not find the words to speak, so I did the next best thing.

I slid my hand beneath Weston's collar, feeling the heat of his flesh on my palm, and pulled him close, crushing my lips against his.

Weston startled for a moment, and

then I heard the faint sound of the microphone dropping to the floor, screeching through the speakers.

Weston's mouth moved smoothly against my own, and he tasted like expensive scotch and broken promises. Somewhere in the back of my mind, I could hear Dawson hollering in the crowd, but I wasn't able to make out what he was saying. I couldn't focus on anything but Weston's tongue in my mouth.

When I broke away, watching as Weston's dark eyes gazed down at me, he steadied me in his arms. The stage lights shone directly in my eyes, and before I could get my full bearings, the DJ called, "That's a wrap!"

"Did I do a good job?" I asked, out of breath.

Though I wasn't sure I was talking about the song anymore.

"You were the best Kiki Dee I've ever seen," Weston said, flashing me a smirk. "Now how about you and I take this show elsewhere," he purred, his voice dark, inviting.

I succumbed to it without question, without hesitation.

"Okay," I breathed as Weston

straightened me, patting me on the back as he pulled his phone out of his pocket, queuing up a ride no doubt.

My heart was in my throat as my pulse raced. I watched as Weston slapped down a wad of bills on the bar, nodding for me to follow him, my heart thudding in my chest.

This is it.

This is where I fall for the man I'll never have.

CHAPTER SIX

Weston

WE BARELY MADE it up the steps, and not because of the alcohol.

Somewhere between the bar and the car ride back to the hotel, Cade flipped a switch. Though I was not complaining one bit, because quite frankly, no one had accosted *me* like that in ages. Usually I'm the one in charge, but I have to say it was kind of nice to be in the spotlight for once.

Cade's mouth worked hungrily on my neck, his tongue sliding against my flesh as he sucked at the tender, taut skin there and I knew he was going to leave a mark, but for the moment, I didn't give a shit. It felt too good, and if Cade's lips on my neck were any indication at how he could work that pretty little mouth, I would have been more than happy to let him suck me like a damn vampire.

I swiped my watch over the hotel lock and it beeped, the mechanism clicking to let us in. I managed to open the door as Cade's lips found their way back to mine, and we barely got two feet in the door before I let my walls down, and finally let myself have a piece of this man.

I slammed Cade's back up against the back of the door with a thud. His eyes were hazy and full of fire and he stared back at me, his golden hair all disheveled, lips all swollen from kissing me, and I took two, slow steps toward him, boxing him against the door with my arms.

"On your knees," I said, my voice thick, and full of lustful command.

Cade stared back at me, pausing for a moment, and a deep growl escaped my throat. I was never a patient man, and the sight of a sweaty, messy Cade only stirred an equal hunger in me.

I slid my right hand up Cade's neck, feeling his pulse, his heated skin, until the edges of my fingers slid into his silky hair. I gripped the locks tightly, showing just a hint of force, a feat that was rather difficult. But I wasn't sure how Cade would respond to such things, and the last thing I wanted to do was scare this perfect man away and go to bed alone.

In my experience, most of the men I'd been with liked the *idea* of power exchange, getting dicked down by the big boss man in charge, but when push came to shove—or more accurately, when I shoved them to the ground and told them who was boss—they usually went soft on me.

This is it. He's either going to hightail his ass out of here or he's going to double down on this cock until I really do make a mess of him.

I dared to hope that he would stay and keep stoking my fire. That he'd be willing to *play.*

Cade's back arched off the door, leaning into my touch as he brought his body against mine, the feel of his rigid hardness against my own was a most welcome answer.

To my surprise, Cade only licked his pouty lips, breathing his words like a prayer.

"Yes, sir." he said haughtily as he took

his time sliding down the floor, his glassy eyes never leaving mine as he did so.

I braced myself as Cade reached for my slacks, wasting no time as he quickly unbuckled my belt and unzipped my pants, shoving them and my briefs down to my ankles in one desperate motion.

"Take off your shirt," I ordered.

Cade looked up at me in question, but did as I asked without hesitation. The hotel light shone down on his fair skin, casting shadows over his defined chest and delicious hipbones. He gazed up at me with glassy, needy eyes, swollen lips begging to be filled with my cock.

I like how he listens to me.

I brought one hand to my freed cock, squeezing and stroking myself slowly, making a show of the motions as I held Cade in place with my gaze. He sat there, perched back on his heels, his knees a fist length apart, frozen to his spot.

Waiting.

Wanting.

This man's a natural sub if I ever saw one.

"Is this what you want, Cade, hmm? Want me to wreck that pretty little mouth of yours until you're singing my name?" I taunted him, watching the heat come alive in his eyes, not missing the way he licked his lips as his gaze settled on my cock.

Cade didn't miss a beat, and I watched as he palmed his own cock through his jeans. The sight flared desire in my blood as his words echoed in the heated silence.

"Yes," he panted. "God, yes."

The desperation in his voice sang to my own hunger, and I groaned in response, a dark chuckle escaping my mouth as I stepped forward, brushing the head of my cock against his swollen, plush lips. Naturally, Cade parted them for me like the hungry man he was, his eyes closing in ecstasy as I teased him, dragging my head over his lips.

I watched in delight as he closed his lips around the tip, kissing, licking me underneath my shaft until I was moaning with pleasure. Normally, I liked to edge myself a bit, but something about the way Cade's lips felt, how his tongue slowly stroked my cock, and the sounds he made as he did so, pushed me into overdrive.

I threaded my hands through his hair, pushing my cock in further, faster, and like the perfect, good boy he was, he opened for me.

Tonight, I don't want to wait.

I want all Cade is willing to give me, and I want it all now.

I thrust my cock through Cade's parted lips, the force only starling him a bit before he eased. Within seconds he was groaning too, licking and sucking me like a damn popsicle on a ninety degree day in the middle of July.

I thrust myself slowly in and out of Cade's warm mouth, feeling the familiar tightening in my balls, and I knew it wouldn't be long.

I could barely contain myself, needing to feel more of the wet, warm sensation of his sweet tortuous mouth, and somehow, almost instinctively, he picked up his pace immediately. I thrust myself with heated force toward the back of Cade's throat as desire took over, taking my right hand and threading my fingers through his soft locks until I'd found my spot behind his head, grasping onto his hair with both hands. All the while coaxing him forward until my cock lodged in the back of his throat and his mouth was flush with my base, until I could hear Cade gag. Stealing a look down at the man choking on my cock, I could see his eyes watering, a bit of drool dripping down his chin, a most wonderful sight.

Fuck, fuck, fuck...

I'm so close...

"That's a good boy," I purred as I watched my cock disappear down Cade's throat once more, hitting that spot that made him gag again, and I was powerless against the sound, the warm, slick feel of his tongue. The sight, the way he looked up at me at that very moment, pushed me over the edge.

I came without warning, gripping him by the hair, holding his head still as I emptied myself down his throat. I watched as his Adams apple bobbed as he swallowed my cum without hesitation, his breathing rapid as he groaned around my cock.

He really is fucking perfect.

A deep rumble escaped my chest as I slowly pulled my cock out of Cade's mouth, letting the remains of my cum coat his beautiful lips, watching as a little bit dripped out of the corners of his precious mouth. A smile formed on my face as I took in my accomplishment.

I wrecked his mouth, just as I promised.

But I'm not done with him. Not by a long shot. Good boys deserve rewards after a job well done.

"Stand up," I ordered, watching as Cade licked my cream off his lips, obeying me without question. The vision of him shirtless, his hands behind his back as he stood in front of me, showcasing the enormous bulge protruding from beneath his tight jeans, was a sight I would never forget.

I pulled him close, wrapping my arm around Cade's exposed waist, feeling the heat of his flesh against my palm. I brought my lips to his ear, whispered my praise.

"You took my cock so good in your mouth, I bet you'd take it even better in that sweet ass."

Cade groaned in response, telling me all I needed to know.

I took his lips without warning, licking him clean of the last bits of myself that clung to his delicious mouth. I slid my hands beneath the waistband of Cade's jeans and boxers, gripping the flesh of his ass tightly, causing him to yelp in my mouth. I rubbed the soft skin for a moment before sliding my hand back out, looping my fingers through the loopholes of Cade's jeans as I tugged him toward me, making our way backward to the bed.

Cade stumbled forward until I caught him, wrapping my arms around his waist as I turned him around until the back of his knees hit the bed. He fell back against the bed with ease, watching me as I removed my shirt, letting it fall to the floor before I hurriedly worked at his jeans. I didn't miss the way his hungry eyes took in my naked form, but this wasn't about *me*. This was about giving Cade the reward he deserved.

I practically ripped the jeans off his body, getting them off so quickly it should have been a damn crime.

But then again, I've had plenty of practice with this sort of thing.

Cade's swollen cock bounced like a spring from the freedom, and I didn't think twice about wrapping my hand around him, feeling the wetness pebbling at his head as he let a groan slip from his lips.

My own cock hardened at the sound, coming back to life slowly but surely, despite the fact I'd just unloaded a round.

But something about this man, this

peachy, sweet as apple pie dream made me want more. I wanted to make him scream my name.

"Please," Cade breathed, his breaths rapid and hot as hell. His cock throbbed in my hand as he thrust his hips desperately against my hand. He flashed his bright eyes at me, pleading for mercy. "Please... let... me..."

"Say it," I egged him on as I continued to spread his wetness over his shaft before bending down to lick the salty liquid leaking out of him, watching his eyes fall shut, his back arching again from my tease.

"Tell me how bad you want to come for me," I said as I continued to lick and kiss his swollen head, angling him further up the bed, so his back was against the headboard.

Cade's knees buckled easily as I nudged them apart, forcing him backward. I took my time as I crawled up the bed, between his legs, my cock suddenly alive and well again, wanting more of this beautiful man begging me to let him come.

Cade's cock throbbed in my hand as I lazily stroked him, the wet, slick sound of my hand sliding over his self-lubricated cock echoing in the silent air.

His head fell back against the pillows as he brought his knees up, planting his feet on the edge of the bed, pushing himself back to give me better access, and a pretty good view of his tight hole.

I took my free hand, sliding my fingers in my mouth one at a time until they'd gathered enough spit, then brought the slick digits to his rim, teasing his entrance.

"Fuck!" He moaned heatedly, his breath starting to turn rapid.

"Wes, please, I—" Cade arched his back off the bed, the way he was panting, begging...

I knew what he wanted.

I slid another finger in, feeling him soften and expand, his dick throbbing as he thrust his hips forward of his own volition, desperate, needing the friction.

I knew exactly what he wanted, and I knew I would give it to him, but a part of me wanted to hear him beg for it.

Beg for *me* to fuck him.

"Say it," I demanded, my tone firm, my voice hitching a octave. "I need to hear you say it," I instructed.

"I need you to make me come, Wes. Please... Fuck..." Cade's voice pleaded, a throaty moan escaping him, causing me to stop for a moment, to take in the sight of him like this. Fingers grasping at the sheets, face all screwed up in agony, pale, sweat-slicked skin glistening in the low incandescent light.

I let go of his cock for the moment, watching as it bobbed back and forth, beads of precum glittering like diamonds in the light as he thrust himself against the air.

I growled, catching Cade's glassy eyes before I dove back in, burying my head between his thighs as I licked him, slathering his clammy skin in a mixture of saliva and sweat, tasting his saltiness mixed with the tartness of his rim until he was writhing beneath me.

"F... fuck... me... I can't... Wes..." he struggled to form words, his voice tinged in unbridled desire.

Please," he huffed out as I lined myself up with his hole.

"Please, I want to come so bad, I—"

I kept my gaze trained on Cade's eyes as I pushed myself in an inch, letting his body acclimate to me. Like the good boy I knew he was, his body welcomed me, gripping my head like a vice and I groaned in response, inching myself in slowly as not to lose my own load. Again.

The sight of Cade's face going slack as I breached his entrance, one torturous inch at a time, was like a religious experience. Or at least it's what I'd imagine a religious experience would be, because I wouldn't know firsthand.

Mama always said I need Jesus. Think I found him in good old Jasper Springs of all places...

When I finally bottomed out, I ran my hand up and down Cade's sweaty chest, feeling his heartbeat as I found my rhythm, as I ground my hips into his. Cade's wet, slick cock left sticky trails along my heated skin as he thrust himself torturously against my stomach.

"Then be a good boy and come for me, Cade," I ordered through my teeth. After my previous orgasm, I knew I wouldn't be able to hold off much longer, either. I'd been with men, and before realizing I was gay, I'd been with a couple women too. But nothing, and no one ever hugged my cock the way Cade's body did, never felt this fucking good. Like he was made for me.

"Come for me," I ordered again, my voice getting just as tight as his insides clutching my cock.

His eyes squinted closed as his face screwed up, and he let out a ragged moan that pushed me over the edge. Cade tightened his thighs around me, and the feel of his warm release coated my abdomen with warmth.

My thrusts came to a halt as I growled out my own groan of satisfaction, spilling myself again as I filled him, all my muscles going soft from the exertion of multiple orgasms. It was no use, and I collapsed on Cade's chest, trying to catch my breath. Elation mixed with alcohol mixed with exhaustion hit me, and I closed my eyes. The faint touch of fingertips grazed along my back, the rhythmic rise and fall of Cade's chest like a lullaby, the sound of his slow and steady breath pulled me into some sort of post-fuck trance. I wasn't certain how long we stayed like that, neither of us moving. When I finally slid out of him, rolling over onto my back, I let sleep overtake me, feeling a sense of wholeness I'd never felt before.

CHAPTER SEVEN

Cade

I WOKE UP to a pounding headache, a sore ass, and an overwhelming need to piss.

A deep, groggy groan escaped me as I reached out my arm to stretch the achy muscles, but my entire body froze when I hit something warm and solid. The touch was like a bucket of cold water as I turned my head in slow motion, my eyes opening wide as my gaze settled on Weston, who was laying on his stomach, naked, with his firm ass on display like a prize-winning statue in a museum. The sunlight that filtered in through the window shone a beam directly on him, and panic settled in.

I lifted up the covers quickly, my suspicions soon confirmed when I saw that I was also naked, and covered in...

Oh, good gravy...

My breath caught in my throat as anxiety flooded me, and I nearly fell over from the shock as I jumped out of bed, in search of the bathroom.

To pee, of course, but also because I needed a moment to process... well, everything.

And because life was apparently as big a fan of Hallmark movies as my mother was, my movement stirred the sleeping, naked man beside me, and just as I made it to the door, his sleepy voice stopped me dead in my tracks, all piss be damned.

"You're up," Weston groaned groggily.

"Uh huh..." I responded, like I'd altogether forgotten the ability to speak like a functional human.

I watched as Weston sat up, noting how the beam of sunlight glistened on his skin, how he ran his hand over his face and through his disheveled, dark hair. My cock twitched, bringing me back to the here and now, reminding me of the magnitude of everything converging on me at once and I jumped into the bathroom, locking the door. In there, I could breathe.

It's fine. You're fine.

Everything's fine...

I made my way to the toilet, realizing as I shook the last bits of piss out, that I was truthfully a sticky, gross mess. My gaze drifted to the stone shower, the door one big see-through pane of glass, and I had to admit a hot shower sounded like just the thing to help clear my head. Just as I was about to turn on the faucet, a slew of images flashed in my brain. Of karaoke kisses, of making out in the car, of Weston's fingers gripping my hair, holding me still while...

I sucked in a breath as the last image came to me, of Weston above me, staring down at me while he...

Oh God.

Did we...

The memory of his tongue, his fingers, his cock filling me made my heart stop.

We did. I let him top me.

Without a condom.

Oh fuck, this... this is not good.

I never sleep with a guy on the first date!

My psyche spiraled as that sarcastic,

bitter part of me chastised myself.

Drinks at Bar Bingo the night you met does not actually count as a date.

"Cade?" Weston's voice pulled me from my thoughts.

"You... okay in there?" he asked, and I could hear the caution in his voice. "I, uh, kind of need to you know—"

I shook my head, turning on the shower, if only because I didn't know what else to do. The sound of his voice alone made me want to melt, to hide until all the doubt and concern dissipated into his warm chest and spicy scent, but I could not face him like this—a god damn anxious mess—not now. Not after...

"Yeah, fine. I'll, uh... be out in a sec," I said as I stepped in the shower, closing the shower curtain. "Just, uh, getting cleaned up," I added, regretting the words immediately, feeling foolish.

God, he must think I'm an idiot...

It didn't take long for me to wash up, as it never did. I never understood how some men could take so long in the shower, when all they had to do was run some shampoo through their hair and some soap over their body.

I watched as the water circled the

drain, feeling the effects of the night of drinking and sex hit me like a sack of potatoes. My stomach flipped as I remembered everything all at once.

Like stumbling like a newborn fawn over Weston as he dragged me through the hotel room, or how I nearly mauled him in the backseat of the car.

You can do this. It isn't like it's your first time. You've got this. Just grab a towel, get dressed, and be on your way. Preserve your dignity.

I nodded to myself as I finished my business, grabbing a towel, and wrapping it around my waist. In the mirror, I could see my own reflection, my messy hair, eyes slightly puffy from a night of bad decisions.

I knew on the other side of the door everything was going to change, and reality would finally sweep in and remind me of the harsh truth that what was arguably the most fun I'd had in a long time, had come to an end.

Still, a part of me wished it could go on a little longer, albeit without the addition of a throbbing headache. For a moment, I thought perhaps I could just stay in the bathroom.

But I knew better.

So instead of hiding in the gorgeous bathroom of Weston's hotel suite, I bravely opened the door to see him standing before me, looking somehow even more delicious with his hair all rumpled, hanging in his jeweled eyes. I didn't want to give in and look at him, because a part of me knew the minute I did, I'd be a goner. I'd never forget him, or the taste of his kiss, the feel of his cock.

I failed miserably as my gaze caught his, and I had to remember to breathe.

Weston sidled past me to do his business, shutting the door and leaving me alone in the light of day. The hotel room didn't look quite as unkempt as one would expect after a night of hot, drunk sex. Though the hurricane inside of me felt every bit unkempt.

I cleared my throat as I took in the sight of the clothes strewn about the floor, like breadcrumbs leading to the bed we'd ended up in. Within seconds, the toilet flushed, and the water echoed, a ticking time bomb to me.

Weston brushed past me once more, grabbing a pair of pants from his suitcase on the way, wasting no time getting dressed. The world around me seemed in slow motion as I gripped my towel around my waist. I watched for a moment as Weston slid his briefs and the tailored pants up over his taut ass, and my cock twitched beneath my towel at the memory of his skin, warm against his own.

I had to look away. If I didn't, I knew somehow I'd make an even bigger fool of myself, so I slowly moved across the room, picking up my discarded clothes as I went, fighting not to steal any more glances at Weston.

If I look at him, I'll see the regret in his eyes, and I don't want to sour this. It's already difficult enough.

Weston must have sensed my anxiety however, because he stopped in front of me just as I was fastening the buttons on my jeans. He dipped his head, catching my gaze from under his lashes.

"Hey," he said calmly, cautiously. The candor of his voice was smooth like chocolate, and just as sinful. The desire to look at him was too hard to fight, and I lost the battle.

"What?" I asked, a lot harsher than I'd meant to. I did not want to see the regret, or the nonchalance on this beautiful man's face as I suffered my own torment. Not when I was spiraling inside over everything that had transpired between us.

The karaoke, the drinks, the sex, the aftermath where we seemed to dance in twilight, buried in the depths of one another for a perfect, blissful moment until we fell asleep.

Together.

"You okay?" Weston asked, his eyebrows furrowed.

An overwhelming desire to soothe the man broiled beneath the surface, despite the fact I felt as if maybe I could use some soothing of my own. The sight of his gaze elicited the truth from my lips. Obeying this man came as second nature, and I knew that should scare me.

So why didn't it?

"I'm fine. I just... don't normally do this... sort of thing," I admitted honestly.

Weston's eyebrows knit together and he looked utterly confused at my words. Like I was speaking French or something.

"What do you mean?" he questioned, legitimately awestruck.

"This," I motioned around the room, between the two of us, who were standing only a hair's breadth away from one another.

When did we get so close...

"The one-night stand thing. I don't normally sleep with men I just met. I, uh... I mean, we, uh... I don't even know if you're—"

"If I'm what?" He looked back at me with confusion.

I could feel my cheeks flush with embarrassment. I forced the word that was on the top of my tongue, out, knowing I was about to completely shatter everything and make it awkward as hell.

"Um... clean."

I watched Weston's eyes widen, as understanding must have dawned on him. He ran a hand over his face, breathing out a sigh.

Fuck, that does it. I've officially ruined the moment.

"I can assure you I take my health more seriously than most," Weston bit out defensively. His response and tone made me feel like a complete idiot, realizing how shitty I must have sounded, how accusatory my tone was, and before I could apologize, tell Weston I wasn't *trying* to be a dick, that I just wanted some reassurance, he looked me dead in the eyes and said, "It's just sex, Cade. It's not like we're getting married, or anything." His tone was even, simple, nonchalant. And all at once, the illusion was broken, along with my weary heart.

Of course, he wouldn't understand. I'm probably just guy number whatever in his travels.

"Obviously," I said, turning away from Weston's smooth, jeweled gaze, feeling like an absolute pile of shit. My head was throbbing, all fantasies and dreams dissolved into thin air.

Reality was a cruel mistress.

The silence between the two of us was deafening as I pulled my shirt back on. Weston looked at me for a moment, before breaking the silence.

"Are you hungry?" he asked warily, as if I were nothing more than a caged animal.

"I'll be fine," I told him, feigning a solidarity I certainly did not feel at the moment.

Last night my walls came down, albeit due to the alcohol, but I'd be damned if I prolonged this only for Weston to pretend he wanted to talk to me, when really he just wanted this awkward moment to be over too.

I pursed my lips as Weston nodded in understanding.

So he can get back to his Sexy Suit Life, doing whatever assholes in sexy suits do.

Drink coffee, run some board meetings. Pick up locals for a night of smoking hot sex.

The memory of Weston's lips at my ear, his words echoing in my brain, 'such a good boy,' echoed like warnings, making my cock twitch and I had to ignore it.

Absolutely not! That is not happening again...

"Do you need a ride?" he questioned as I watched him pull a fresh suit jacket on. He did not look at me directly again, instead just focused on putting on his watch, which looked like a brand new Movado.

Just because I live in Jasper Springs doesn't mean I don't fashion. I've been oogling one of those since Christmas.

"No, I'm good, thanks," I answered as I pulled out my phone.

Six missed calls and texts from Dawson.

Did James Bond murder you?

I tapped out a reply quickly, focusing for the moment on something that wasn't Weston.

The only thing he murdered is my dreams.

I kept my gaze trained on the screen as the bubbles popped up, and Dawson responded immediately.

That bad huh? You need me to call you? Pretend there's a family emergency?

His words made me feel a little better. It wouldn't be the first time Dawson would have had to come pick me up from a night of bad ideas with bad for me assholes.

Not to mention, he was one of them at one time.

I tapped out my reply almost immediately, thankful for the save.

Actually can you give me a ride to work?

Dawson answered fast, clearly prepared.

Of course. Not like I have any cats in trees to save.

He added some cat emojis for good measure.

I tapped back a thumbs up with the address of the Palisades Hotel.

"Well, it's been fun, but... I, uh... gotta go. Work... and stuff," I said quietly.

Weston slid his hand in his jacket pocket, his expression emotionless. He shrugged. "I get it. See you around, Cade."

"See ya," I answered as I headed out the door and down toward the lobby in search of something sweet to soak up all the shame, guilt, and sadness in my system while I waited for Dawson to get me.

CHAPTER EIGHT

Cade

WHEN DAWSON'S CANDY apple red truck pulled up to the curb, I crawled in, waiting for the judgment I knew was coming.

Better to just get it over with.

But instead, Dawson only handed me a clean *Jasper Springs Fire Co.* long-sleeve, a large iced coffee, and a bag with a donut.

Chocolate glazed, my favorite.

"You're a lifesaver," I breathed with relief as my stomach growled.

You'd think the Palisades would have had something unhealthy, but the cafe was stocked with nothing but Nutrigrain bars.

"Figured you'd need to eat your feelings a little bit, you sounded a little stressed. Plus, I'm sure you feel like shit."

"You don't know the half of it," I mumbled as I took a long drink of iced coffee. The sweetness was overpowering, but it made me feel a little better at the moment.

"Did you at least have fun?" Dawson asked with that annoying tone of his, the one that used to get on my nerves, but now I'd become numb to hearing.

I stared out the window, chewing my straw as we took off. Jasper Springs was already bustling as the shops opened and the traffic had started. Stealing a glance at the clock, I noted it was nearly nine thirty.

I usually don't sleep so late...

Thank God I'm working the afternoon shift today.

"Yeah, I guess," I answered with a sigh as I shifted in the passenger seat.

It wasn't a lie. I *did* have fun. A little too much fun.

"I mean, when I left, you two were practically dry humping each other on stage, and you were giggling up a storm, so..." Dawson teased me, raising his eyebrows.

I knew he wouldn't stop until he'd gotten every sordid detail like the pain in the ass he was, but after my disaster of a morning, I just didn't have the spoons to rehash everything and feel worse than I already did.

"I don't want to talk about it, Dawson," I said, my heart breaking a little as the memories hazily replayed in my brain on repeat. In truth, I didn't want to talk about it, or even think about it.

The memory of Weston's lips, of his salacious tongue, and his cock would be tattooed on my damn brain for eternity.

Along with my stupidity.

Real smooth, Cade.

I half expected Dawson to push for details like he always did, forgoing boundaries altogether, but to my surprise he did no such thing. Instead, his gaze softened.

"Maybe you should take the day off," he suggested.

It wasn't a bad idea, but I knew being at home all cooped up would have only given my anxiety full reign to focus on all the spots I'd fucked everything up. No, I needed to move. To keep my mind busy so I wouldn't think of Weston and his gorgeous green eyes and sweet, chocolatey voice. Plus, there was the fundraiser the hospital was doing with Rhodes Enterprises, which we'd been planning for months and the hospital would be understaffed today because of it.

"I can't," I responded, watching the world pass me by. "The pet hospital is spread thin as it is today with the fundraiser, and a hangover with a side of guilt isn't exactly a reason to call off. At least, it isn't to me."

I expected Dawson to refute, to argue with me about how a hangover most certainly counted as a sick day, but he didn't. Instead, he just turned up the radio and left me to wallow in my own self-pity like the loser I felt I truly was at the moment.

Just once, I'd like things to work out instead of blowing up in my face.

CHAPTER NINE

Cade

I SUCKED DOWN another pull of my iced coffee as I headed into work, only to see my boss, Diane, flustered at the main desk. The ever-present cacophony of meows and barks was like music to my ears, and the caffeine was doing a bit to lift my spirits. I didn't feel a hundred percent better, but I did feel functional.

That had to count for something, right?

"Afternoon, Diane," I said in my best, chipper, customer service voice. Somewhere in the distance, a cockatoo cawed loudly.

"Oh, thank goodness you're here,

Cade," she exclaimed with exasperation as she looked at the clock. 'And you're early! Bless you!" she said, rounding to the front of the desk, appraising me with a look that made my blood chill.

Oh no, I know that look.

"Ricardo had to leave early this morning, with a stomach bug," she said, batting her eyelashes at me.

No, no, no...

"Oh, that sucks," I deadpanned, even though my mind was screaming, "back away from the boss... slowly... find something to stock... fast."

"I need you to head down to Charlestown Street and work the booth." She clasped her fists together, doing her best impression of a puppy dog from those awful Sarah McLachlan commercials.

"Diane, you know I don't do events..." I started to say, but she pouted.

Of course she knew that, but the use of puppy dog eyes meant she was screwed and had no other option.

Fuck.

"Please, Cade, I don't have anyone else. Terri's worked six days this week and it's her daughter's school play today," Diane said, laying on the whining real thick.

I hated to say no, especially when my five foot two frazzled gremlin boss looked at me like I was her damn knight in shining armor.

Maybe the fresh air will do me good...

I sighed, admitting defeat.

"Fine." I huffed regrettably. "But I'm going to need to go home first and get my car. Dawson dropped me off," I touted. Diane didn't miss a beat.

"Oh! You are the best Cade! Thank you so much!" she said with so much appreciation I almost felt bad for wanting to decline. Almost.

I nodded, forcing a smile as I pulled out my phone and texted Dawson once more, telling him everything that had transpired in the ten minutes since he dropped me off.

He's going to kill me.

Like the best wingman he was though, Dawson tapped back a reply within seconds.

Lucky for you, I didn't make it very far. I ran into Lois at the post office and she talked my fucking head off for five minutes straight. I just walked out the door. Coming to get you."

For the second time in an hour, Dawson had saved my ass, and so I sent another thumbs up.

It was going to be a long day.

CHAPTER TEN

Weston

I SIGHED AS the door closed with a resounding echo. This was the part I loathed the most, the thing that I couldn't seem to change about my life.

The lonely morning when everyone walked away.

I'd been single for far too long, grown accustomed to the way of life of a bachelor, and on most days with enough alcohol and enough money, I could pretend it was all fine, that I was content with the way things were. But as I watched Cade's delicious ass leave the hotel room, I felt the petulant void inside of me grow.

Can't even keep them for breakfast anymore.

The phone rang, pulling me from my misery. I didn't even have to look to know who was calling, as the Darth Vader march sounded in the cavernous room.

I answered regrettably, clearly not in the mood to deal with anything but my own wallowing.

"What?" I growled, my tone much harsher than I truly meant it to be.

"Please, tell me you've left the hotel already," my mother said dryly.

"I'm leaving in five minutes, mother," I huffed whilst straightening my suit, running a hand through my hair to even it out.

The sunlight filtered in through the window, lighting up the room in its sweet, golden glow. Though despite all its golden rays, I couldn't help but feel gloomy in comparison.

Shitty way to start the day, but I guess I shouldn't be surprised.

"Where are you staying?" she pressed.

"It doesn't matter. This damn town is tinier than shit. I'll be there in fifteen minutes, tops."

"That doesn't answer my question,"

she huffed.

"If you must know, I'm staying at the Palisades."

"That's at least a twenty-five minute drive, Weston!"

I waved my hand at the air as I took my time grabbing my wallet, sliding it into my pants.

"It's going to be a thirty minute drive if you don't get off this phone with me and let me call an Uber."

"Do take this seriously, dear. This event is important to the company," she said with a sigh.

And the guilt trip starts. Barely been here twenty-four hours, that's got to be a record.

"It's important you understand we do more than just sell products, honey. Our strength is with this community."

"Of course, I wouldn't want to put a damper on the *company*," I drawled sarcastically.

"It is important to your father, too. And me," she said quietly.

"Uh huh, of course," I responded, hurrying to put an end to the conversation before it became the one I always dreaded hearing.

Because no matter how many times I told my parents, it never seemed to sink in.

I didn't *want* to run Rhodes Enterprises. The very idea of being cooped up in board meetings and overseeing spreadsheets sounded like the opposite of living to me.

It wasn't like I'd never worked before. In fact, up until a year ago I would have rather loved to stay at my job at the Men's Warehouse, even though it wasn't my family's idea of a genuine job. It was just shitty timing. We'd all been downright shocked when the place closed, or 'relocated', and I hadn't been asked to move with the staff I'd grown close to.

Ever since I'd been in limbo, trying to find something, anything—or someone— to pull me out of the stasis my life had become. It seemed almost as if there was nothing truly constant in my life except the inevitable change I did not seek, and a future I didn't ask for.

"Weston—"

"Leaving now, mother. See you soon," I said, not bothering to wait for her to chime in and say her goodbyes before hanging up on her as I walked out the door of the lonely, silent room, and into the overwhelmingly beige hallway of the Palisades, dreading the stupid fundraiser I'd been tasked with.

CHAPTER ELEVEN

Weston

THE SUN WAS at its peak as I strolled through the blocked off streets of town. Jasper Springs itself wasn't a large town, but the Main Street stretch alongside Charleston Street was big enough to make even the occasional passerby wonder if Jasper Springs was larger than it looked. There were several tents strewn along the streets, everything from vegan food trucks and popsicle stands, to a multitude of small businesses like Taylor Made Bouquets and Penn's Bakery, the bakery my mother loves, as well as the local community staples such as the Jasper

Springs Volunteer Fire Co. and the Jasper Springs Pet Hospital.

"Don't be such a stick in the mud," my mother nipped as we strolled down Main Street, stopping in front of a food truck selling donut holes and homemade poptarts.

"I am not a stick in the mud," I retorted, wrinkling my face at her tone.

"You've been scowling ever since you showed up, my dear. If your skincare routine wasn't handpicked by Francesca, I'd worry about you getting wrinkles from that incessant frown."

I rolled my eyes. Nothing ever got past this woman, I swear.

"I'm just... it was a rough morning." I chewed on my lip, wishing I hadn't said anything the moment the words left my mouth.

My mother's eyes lit up with resounding judgment. She'd snared me in her trap, again.

"Stay out past your bedtime again?" she nipped, her tone sweet yet full of venom at the same time.

My mother, Hilaria Rhodes, was quite capable of getting even the toughest soldier to dispel their secrets. I'd watched her on many occasions when we'd attended a plethora of events.

"I haven't had a bedtime since the third grade, mother."

Her phone rang, dissolving the moment and her attention, and I thanked my lucky stars. She answered her phone immediately, holding up a hand to me, if only to brush me off for something far more pressing. Perhaps someone had a more dramatic situation that needed judgment than just her reluctant son.

I was more than familiar with the life of my socialite mother though, and therefore, I knew there would be no better time to exit than the one moment I'd been given. So I smiled and nodded as she turned away, spouting off "No, Cynthia', and 'that will not do', and 'please ask Mr. Lammie."

I did not waste my moment, taking my leave as I ambled down Charleston Street alone, checking out the booths one by one. The sun beat down on my back, causing steam to heat my skin beneath my shirt.

And that was when I saw him, though to be fair I wasn't entirely sure I hadn't imagined a mirage from the dire heat.

Cade stood behind one of the booths, dressed in a pink polo shirt, smiling that bright Jasper Springs smile. *Jasper Springs Pet Hospital* was sprawled across the banner in stark white font, little pawprints bespeckling the bright blue tablecloth. A part of me wanted to casually stroll over and strike up a conversation, even though Cade had made it clear he wanted nothing to do with me after this morning.

But there was also a part of me that was terrified of being caught staring, at being caught wishing for something more.

Just this once.

CHAPTER TWELVE

Cade

I HAD JUST gotten done setting up the Jasper Springs Pet Hospital booth, when Regina, one of the firewomen from Dawson's firehouse—who was conveniently set up next to me—whacked me in the arm.

"What the hell, Gina..."

"The prodigal son returns," she deadpanned, and I huffed in annoyance.

"What the hell are you talking about?" I asked. Being as close to Dawson as I was, I was more than familiar with a handful of the firefighters from the firehouse, though I didn't consider many of them my friends like I did with Dawson.

However, Gina Corolla didn't seem to be phased by my lack of social skills.

What were the odds the firehouse would be set up next to the pet hospital booth anyway?

"Haven't you heard about the Rhodes' very hot, very single, and very gay son?" She looked at me with question.

I avoided her gaze, choosing instead to straighten out some brochures on my table.

"You know I don't keep up on town gossip," I said. And it was true. I'd never cared for the secret whispers and looks, the currency of small town suburbia, and I certainly didn't want to end up a whisper on someone's tongue myself.

No, I preferred to keep my life more than private, and I respected others rights to do the same.

"Well, since you've been living under a damn rock, he's coming this way so you can get a good look at him."

"Gina..." I protested, but all she did was turn my head in the direction of...

Holy shit.

Is that Weston?

"Twelve o'clock sharp. With the blue shirt, rolled up sleeves."

I felt my entire body freeze on sight.

Weston strolled down the street lazily, hands in his pockets, his blue shirtsleeves rolled up to the elbow only showcasing his fresh sun-kissed glow. His dark hair blew about in the wind, and I could have sworn I heard angels singing.

Or demons, more accurately given the state of things.

"He's..."

"Hotter than a fucking rack of ribs straight from the grill, I know," Gina said with excitement as my mind short circuited.

Rhodes.

Weston.

Weston Rhodes.

Heir to Rhodes Enterprises.

This can't be happening!

At that very moment, our eyes met just like in the movies. Weston stopped dead in his tracks, a light smirk coursing over his lips.

"You should totally ask him out," Gina cooed behind me.

I swallowed nervously as the memories of the previous night of passion flooded my brain, causing my damn cock to spring to life.

Again.

I cleared my throat as I turned away from Weston's smoldering gaze, fussing over anything else I could to try and regain a semblance of order once again. Because at the moment, all I could think about was how badly I'd messed up that morning, noting that Weston would likely want nothing to do with me now.

Now, I was just an embarrassment.

"Yeah, I don't think so. Weston is so far out of my league we're not even in the same ballpark," I chided.

Gina's lips curled into a smile. "I never said his name was Weston..."

And that was the moment Mitchell and Dawson arrived at the firehouse booth.

Perfect timing, as always.

I watched as Weston talked to a group of women, smiling genuinely and schmoozing like the unabashed rich kid he obviously was, feeling a pang in my heart. I forcibly tore my gaze from him, if only to try and put the beautiful man—and the memory of his cock down my throat—out of my mind.

"You look good for hungover," Mitchell said as he snapped a photo of me, not giving a shit if I was ready or not.

I swatted at my 'friend with camera', as Dawson let out a laugh.

"What the hell are you doing here?" I asked, with about as much venom as a daddy-long-legger. They are actually venomous, but their fangs are too short to actually hurt anyone.

What can I say, arachnids are my spirit animal.

Dawson smiled with mischief. "Sarge said I should come down here to sign calendars."

Gina rolled her eyes. "Please, like anyone would actually want you to sign anything."

Dawson opened his arms wide, motioning to himself like he was some great, Herculean hero.

To be fair, in his own brain he probably is.

"Want to take a wager on that, G?" he asked as some girls walked past, giggling as they took a gander at him. Against the bright red banner, he looked every bit Mister March, and he liked to remind everyone he was the *hottest* fireman on the calendar every chance he got.

Gina shook her head. "You're a fucking idiot."

"I am, but... I'm a hot idiot," he chimed as Mitchell snapped another photo.

"Any new recruits yet, G?" Dawson asked as he shifted his stance, brushing off his charm and turning to business.

"Not yet, but the day is still young," she said with a shrug.

Dawson nodded at me, glancing at Weston with that look that I knew was trouble.

"What are the odds..." he said with a smile.

"Dawson, don't..." I begged. I knew Dawson well enough to know he would make a scene just to get Weston over here, just so he could push my buttons.

Even if he thought he was helping.

"Isn't that the guy you were singing with last night at karaoke?" Mitchell asked as he snapped a photograph of Weston, who was now checking out Sandra's Homemade Candles & Candies booth.

"It is," Dawson answered before I could even speak for myself.

"Shut up! You did not karaoke with *Weston freaking Rhodes?*" Gina said in mock-shock.

Instantly, anxiety flooded me and I felt

as if I wanted to crawl under the table to avoid this whole conversation.

"Wait... that's Weston *Rhodes*?" Mitchell asked in surprise.

"Who?" Dawson asked, clueless as usual. For a man who loved to know everything, he was always somehow the last to know the town gossip, despite being in the middle of it all the time.

"The heir to Rhodes Enterprises, Dawson. You know, the tech guys who upgraded our entire security system, the very company whose idea it was to *put* this fundraiser together..." Gina gaped at him.

Dawson only had to audacity to blink like a sleepy kitten, the gears in his head obviously working overtime.

I felt as if I was truly going to be sick. But perhaps it was just the fact I hadn't eaten anything more than a donut and twenty ounces of iced coffee this morning.

Dawson whistled, a laugh escaping his throat. "Nice catch, Cade." he said, flashing me a wink.

"Does he have a big dick?" Mitchell teased, cracking a smile.

"Oh my God, Cade, did you two—" Gina chimed in, and the heat rose up my neck into my cheeks, betraying any words I might say to try and save my dignity.

I was rather flustered and all I could do was shift my stance, trying my hardest not to focus on the fact that Weston was walking over to *my booth.*

"I do not kiss and tell," I snapped.

Mitchell let out a laugh as Dawson childishly taunted him, Gina's 'oh my God's' coming out more like guinea pig squeals.

Kill me now.

"That is a resounding yes!" she teased, and the mortification set in as the blood rushed to my cheeks.

I need to change this conversation right now, or I need to—

"Mr. Rhodes, so nice to meet you!" Mitchell said far too cheerfully in my opinion, pulling me from my internal meltdown.

Weston stood only a few feet away, all long legs and tailored suits, his dark hair hanging in his dark, sexy eyes, and I couldn't help but stare at the *hot as hell* heir to one of the most successful businesses in Jasper Springs, feeling frozen in place once again.

No one made the world fall away

around me quite like this man, and that made me feel both alarmed and... hopeful.

Weston turned his head only slightly, smirking at me before turning to Mitchell, shaking his hand firmly.

"Good to meet you too, sir," he said politely, with that same decadent smoothness that made my insides melt.

"Mind if I get some pictures of you for the paper?" Mitchell said with a grin that was far too mischievous for my liking.

Oh no, I know that look...

"Of course, just tell me where you'd—"

"Cade you can stand here, and Mr. Rhodes—" Mitchell had gone into photographer mode as he ordered about, pointing to the spots and structuring his photo. My blood ran cold, and a part of me wanted to murder him.

"You can stand here," Mitchell said with a smile as he placed me next to Weston.

I shot him a murderous gaze, if only to let him know I knew exactly what he was doing. He and Dawson were so meddlesome sometimes, but I knew I wouldn't refuse him. Whether or not he really was going to use this photograph for the paper or not, I knew Mitchell *did* in fact need photos for the paper, which would no doubt be running an article on this fundraiser. Not to mention, I would look like an asshole if I protested, and I didn't want Weston to think I was an even bigger asshole.

Why does that bother me?

Sure, we had spent the night together, but Weston had been more than clear it didn't mean anything to him.

I didn't mean anything to him.

Except, it *did* mean something to me, but I couldn't show that. At best, I'd just look like an overly needy stage five clinger, which is just as bad if not worst than being an asshole.

So if it meant nothing to him, I should act as if it meant nothing to me, too.

No, I wouldn't let my inner clinger out in front of Weston Rhodes, the man whose gaze made my damn cock twitch from just his proximity, and certainly not in front of the firehouse gossipers, and a meddling photographer.

So I swallowed my pride and my feelings as I stood where Mitchell directed, on the left in front of the banner. There was a small modicum of space between Weston and I, which I pretended not to notice.

Even though I could feel the heat steaming between us...

Mitchell snapped his picture, taking a moment to review it before looking up with a smile and winking at me.

I'm totally going to murder him for this later.

"Okay, that's good, but this time I'm going to need you two to get a little closer. A little more... comfortable," he said.

Dawson giggled in the background, and Gina smacked him.

"Of course," Weston said smoothly as he scooted closer to me, leaving just a hair of space between us. The scent of his cologne invaded my airways, and made my stomach do a little flip.

I'm so fucked.

"Cade, move in a little bit," Mitchell instructed, and my jaw immediately tensed. Yet I did as Mitchell asked. The movement put Weston and I side by side, and I had to fight the desire to look at him.

To look up into his beautiful gem-like eyes and fall under his spell yet again.

But I didn't *have* to look at him to fall under his spell, apparently. Just being close to him was enough.

Just as Mitchell set to take his picture, Weston's smooth, velveteen voice purred in my ear, "Such a good boy," and I knew I was was absolutely doomed.

CHAPTER THIRTEEN

Weston

"THANKS, MR. RHODES," the photographer said, but I could not entirely focus on the paparazzi at the moment. Growing up under my mother's socialite arm meant I could pose and smile and deal with photographers in my damn sleep, even on my worst days.

But all I could do was replay the last twelve or so hours in my brain, to remember to breathe, as standing next to Cade was driving me and my unruly dick bananas.

"Of course," I said politely, noticing that Cade had not moved from my side.

It's a start...

I watched the photographer make his way over to the booth next to us, chatting up the two firefighters he obviously knew, likely for a picture.

For the moment, I had Cade to myself.

"Feeling better?" I asked smoothly. Almost as if Cade had suddenly remembered my presence, he shook his head, a blush creeping onto his cheeks that reminded me of his flushed cheeks during our initial karaoke session.

His pale skin looked quite beautiful with such tones, making me think of plenty of other areas of skin I'd like to see tinged pink. My dick twitched at the thought, but I managed to keep my face plain, even.

Cool as a cucumber.

"I, um... guess you could say that," Cade said as he leaned against the table, his gaze dancing around the busy streets, focusing on anything but me.

It's almost as if I make him nervous...

At that very moment, Cade's stomach let out a rumble that was impossible to ignore.

"You are a terrible liar, *Cade,*" I said, liking the way his name sounded on my tongue. I wanted to say it as much as I could.

Cade crossed his arms. "Well, I'd feel better if you stopped staring at me like... like..."

I had to admit I liked seeing him all flustered, and I couldn't help but play his adorable game, so I leaned against the booth languidly, fighting a smile.

"Like what?" I whispered darkly, watching as his gaze dipped to my lips.

"Like I'm a damn piece of meat, for starters," Cade bristled, though his tone wasn't angry or aggravated. Instead, it was full of unspoken things, and even carried a hint of embarrassment.

Did this darling little morsel not know how delicious he actually was?

Obviously not.

I cocked my head to the side. "I can assure you, as I've tasted the best meat the world has to offer, you do not fall into the category of average meat."

I watched as Cade's eyebrows furrowed, almost as if he was somehow hurt by my words.

I don't understand...

I wasn't sure if it was something I said, or perhaps if it was just the fact that he was feeling unwell at the moment, clearly as starved as I was. The heat of this damn town would make anyone lust for sustenance.

"Although, I must say I am quite famished myself. Perhaps we could actually... grab something to eat?" I offered.

A deep part of me that was foreign until this moment bubbled up with the innate desire to *take care* of this man, show him just how prized and fine he was, because perhaps no one else had ever done such a thing.

All at once, I watched the sparkle return to Cade's eyes at my offer.

"I, uh... I am kind of hungry, but I can't exactly *leave* my post," he said, chewing his lip. The sight was somehow both endearing and hot as hell as instant images of me *biting* at that lip until he begged me to stop filled my brain.

Focus, Weston!

Of course he can't just abandon his post.

Clearly this man messes with my ability to think straight...

"I could grab you something if you tell me what you want," the words came out somehow huskier than I'd intended them, and my mouth had gone dry.

"You, uh... you don't *have* to do that," Cade said sweetly as he ran a hand through his hair.

"And why not?" I asked, confused once more. This man was sending me very mixed signals. I looked at him, puzzled.

"I know I wasn't exactly the most, um... I mean, I kind of—"

"If this is about what happened between us, I can assure you I'm not offering to grab you food just because we had sex," I insisted.

It was true. Granted, I *wanted* to have a repeat of the other night, but this moment wasn't about that. I didn't feel an obligation to buy this man lunch just because we'd had a steamy roll in the hay. I wanted to buy this man lunch because ever since I couldn't get him out of my head, and I wanted to know more about the man who had vexed me so.

Though to be fair, it would have been something I would have done in the past to placate those I once shared my bed with—the polo riders or the designers and artists who'd often wanted to be spoiled even if it was for a night only, purely because they knew I had the means to do so and that was my reputation back home. As if there was something *wrong* with wanting someone to spoil, hoping that if I threw enough money or gifts around, maybe, just maybe one of them would want to stay with *me.*

Somehow, as Cade's words fell over me, I knew this was different, though I couldn't explain why or how I knew. It wasn't about the sex, not really. I genuinely felt a need, a desire to take care of this man, this adorable, blue-eyed darling who was almost as skittish as a mouse.

To... *comfort him.*

I wanted to make Cade feel better, wanted to see a legitimate smile on his beautiful face.

What was the harm in that?

However well meaning I'd been, Cade's shoulders tightened at my words.

How could I make this man understand, I was only trying to help?

To reassure him one thing did not equal another?

I could separate a man from his dick, even if I didn't do it often.

"I mean, we were both sort of drunk, and it was great, but... One thing doesn't have anything to do with the other, I promise," I said, trying my best to comfort him even though I was not good at such a thing.

"Oh," Cade said, his voice getting a tad quieter.

"Tell you what," I said, not liking the strange tension that had befallen us, "You stay here, and I will hunt you... er... us... down something fried and sweet, and we can put this whole... debacle behind us. Start fresh." I pushed away from the table lightly, capturing his weary gaze.

Cade looked up at me, his blue eyes searching mine for something I was not sure of.

Answers maybe?

"Yeah, sure," Cade said, but his smile did not reach his eyes, and as I wandered off in search of sustenance, only to be pulled away once more by the inevitable devil that awaited me—my father—I hoped I would find a way to make things up to Cade.

CHAPTER FOURTEEN

Cade

I STEPPED THROUGH the front door, nearly exhausted from the events of the last twenty-four hours.

I wasn't sure why I expected Weston to come back with anything. After all, I knew assholes like Weston Rhodes didn't really do the 'nice guy' thing. They didn't treat you to a smorgasbord of breakfast or buy you coffee just because they wanted to talk to you or enjoy your company.

Which makes him no different than any other asshole you've gotten your hopes up for.

I nonchalantly tossed my keys in the bowl by the door after locking it, the silence of my humble abode thick and disheartening. The lights came on of their own accord, and it was all I could do to stand there and think that maybe this was as good as it would get. Maybe I truly was meant to be a small town man, living a small town life in my quiet, quaint house, eating rocky road ice cream on the couch forever whilst watching reruns of my favorite shows.

As if perfectly on cue, my stomach grumbled once more, and I tossed the box of pizza I had picked up at Jasper Springs Pizza on the way home on the counter. Popping the lid, the scent of salty pepperoni and sweet tomato sauce filled my senses, making my mouth water. I set about to finding myself a plate, a glass of lime seltzer soda, and of course, a pint of ice cream.

I kicked off my shoes, discarding my well-worn and sweaty shirt on the arm of the couch before curling up in the cushions with my culinary treasures, and turned on the tv. Suddenly, all the exhaustion and stress slithered off of my shoulders as I got lost in the electric light, practically inhaling my food as the comfortable air conditioning soothed my hot, tired muscles.

Though nothing seemed to erase the memory of being on stage with Weston, or the way his lips turned up in a smile as he kissed me, sliding his tongue into my mouth.

Or the way he had *commanded* me to get on my knees, the way his words of praise made me feel.

Good boy.

The memory of the prior night danced with that of the earlier afternoon, when Mitchell had tormentingly posed us together for a picture I still wasn't entirely sure *was* for the paper, but a part of me appreciated the gesture, nonetheless, even if at the time I'd felt wary.

The memory of the heat from Weston's breath on my skin caused my blood to rush through my veins, and his whispered words incited a desire deep within me that no one else had ever been truly capable of igniting.

I wanted to be *good* for a man, but no man had ever seen me as good *enough.*

Not until...

I leaned my head back, hitting the back of my couch as my cock throbbed from the memory.

Fucking hell.

I sighed, knowing there was no use.

So instead of combating my cock, which had a mind of its own, instead, I slid my hand beneath the waistband of my pants, fully intending to adjust my erection for the moment so I could finish my damn ice cream, but the touch did nothing to soothe me. In fact, it only made the need to come that much worse.

I groaned in annoyance, my voice tinged with desperation as I focused my gaze on the ceiling.

I knew I should forget Weston Rhodes, Hottie-Mc-Hot-Suit, the man of my damn rom-com dreams. But in the privacy of my own home, I could submit to the meddlesome desire, the fantasies that shamelessly plagued me.

So I gave in.

I popped the button on my jeans, unzipping my pants if only to let my strained cock breathe. I breathed a sigh of relief as my solid cock sprung forth like a damn spring, thick and wanting, already pebbling with moisture as I let my eyelids fall shut. I licked my lips as I let Weston's smooth voice reverberate in my brain.

"Good boy."

I wrapped my hand around my sensitive head, spreading some of my moisture along my engorged shaft, letting the rest of the memories out of their cage.

"You took my cock so good in your mouth," the words echoed like a canyon as I gripped my shaft, pulling and tugging slowly, building a rhythm.

I continued to let my thoughts wander down the dark pathway of memory, remembering just how Weston's thick, solid cock felt as it hit the back of my throat, causing me to gag.

None of the men I had ever been with had ever made me *gag*.

I'd panicked only slightly at first, at the feeling of losing my breath, but when I looked up to see Weston and his dreamy eyes full of lust and pleasure, I couldn't deny the sight was most appealing.

And so I hollowed my cheeks, and slid my mouth over Weston's cock until my eyes watered and the feeling of choking prevailed, reveling in the rush of his sweet release as he gripped my hair, fists tightening as he spilled himself down my throat. And like the needy man I was, I swallowed every drop, relishing in the sound of his moans and groans.

My breath caught in my throat as the thoughts fueled me and my impending release.

"Such a good boy."

The memory of Weston's whispers on my skin from this afternoon meshed with the memory of his wet and warm tongue, laving at my tight entrance, licking, nibbling at my sensitive skin, bathing me in warm saliva.

I thrust my swollen cock into my hand, some desperate liquid escaping, coating my shaft and hand. I didn't waste a drop, taking the warm wetness, slathering it over my tip and shaft like sticky, warm lube, my hand and hips picking up a rhythm as I chased my orgasm through the clouds and haze of memory. My thrusts came harder, my hips moving faster as my breathing intensified, as I thrust my cock desperately against my warm, wet palm.

"Come for me, Cade."

I pumped my cock, feeling the release nearly instantly as I remembered just how Weston had ordered me to come, and how I had obeyed, almost as if my body understood far better than my brain did, that I would do *anything* for this man. I would do whatever he asked.

I had been *so good.*

Wet, thick ropes of warm cum sprayed onto my exposed abdomen, some sliding down over my hands as I fought to control the amount or the trajectory of my release and catch my breath. I opened my eyes and stared at the ceiling with a mixture of remorse, regret, and desire that left me both sated and hungrier than I'd ever been before.

The movie credits rolled on the television, and I basked in its artificial glow, exhaustion overcoming me with finality.

CHAPTER FIFTEEN

Weston

I COULD NOT stop thinking about that damn fundraiser. Or more accurately, the adorable puppy-dog-eyed vet technician who caused my blood to rush just from his proximity.

I ran a hand over my face, sighing before taking a long drink of my *Oban*, remembering Cade's sweet, somehow endearing flirtations.

Oban-Wan Kenobi is pretty catchy.

Though I had to admit, the fundraiser was far from my element. When I'd agreed to show up, play the part my parents wished, I'd thought I would have endless time to waltz around, smile and kick back for a change.

But it seemed that was the furthest thing from my parent's agenda. Once my mother had discovered me, again, she'd sunk her perfectly manicured claws into my arm for the remainder of the event, buffalo fries be damned.

Time had droned on as I was shuffled from associate to associate, and before I knew it, I was both hungry and disappointed.

When I'd finally been dismissed from my duties, the Jasper Springs Pet Hospital booth was gone, as was the firefighter's booth.

I'd been too late, and I silently cursed my parents for once again throwing a monkey wrench in my plans.

Into my entire life, if we're counting.

I'd thought perhaps maybe I just needed to get out of the damned sleepy little town. Maybe getting away from Jasper Springs would dispel the thoughts of Cade from my mind. Outside of his radius, maybe I could think straight, and so I took off to the famed Sedona, without a second thought.

The restaurant itself lay between the city and Jasper Springs and somehow blended sweet, southern home cooking and upscale gastropub meets French cuisine; a combination that should not have worked at all, but together was absolutely magical.

But not even a full-bodied Scotch and filet could fill the void I felt in my heart, my soul.

What the hell is wrong with me?

Just as I aimed to sip the remains of my second glass, my phone chirped a familiar chime.

Jamie.

"Hello?" I answered, leaning back in my chair, waiting for the onslaught that I knew was about to come.

Jamie did not disappoint as she launched off into a tirade about one of our former coworkers, who happened to be the on again, off again man in her life.

"I told you, he is an asshole, darling. I tried to warn you," I said. At this point, I felt like a broken record sometimes.

"Save it, Wes. We both know we prefer our men emotionally damaged and unavailable."

Ah, so it's off again.

"I do not *prefer* emotionally damaged men or unavailable men. I just seem to attract them like a damn magnet. It's not my fault I am who I am."

Jamie hummed on the other end of the phone. " And who are you lusting after right now? Some small town hottie who's *'never done this before'*." She snickered.

Naturally, I guffawed at her insinuations.

One time, Jamie... one time.

"I'll have you know, Cade is not—"

"So there is someone," Jamie sing-songed.

Damn it.

Weston you are smarter than this. You walked right into that!

I rolled my eyes, chastising myself for falling into Jamie's trap. I stared at the ornate venetian glass chandelier, contemplating lying or coming clean to my former coworker slash closest thing I had to a best friend.

"There was a night, Jamie. That's all. It's hardly anything to make a fuss over." I said the words, but after two rounds of scotch, I wasn't sure I believed them entirely myself.

"But you wanted a morning, am I right? Maybe even a lunch the next day? Someone to commiserate with while you play good son to mommy and daddy?"

Why isn't this woman a shrink?

"Even if I did want those things, Jamie, the chances are slim. He... *Cade*... doesn't seem to want anything to do with me."

"You said chances were slim, Wes. Not impossible. Besides, a man who doesn't succumb to your money and model looks? Shit, I'd want him too."

I sneered in response to her taunting, and just as I was about to speak, Jamie's laughter subsided, giving way to a pregnant pause.

"Why do you think he wants nothing to do with you? Did you say something? Was the sex bad? Did you get whiskey dick or—"

My shoulders fell, and thanks to the alcohol in my system, the words came of their own volition as I confessed my sins to a woman who was certainly not pure enough to take confession.

"No, it was... wonderful, despite the alcohol, but—"

Jamie waited for me to continue, and for once in my life, I felt the need to unload, to give some of what I'd been carrying around up.

To vent, and trust my friend with the

truth.

"The next morning... *this morning*... he seemed to be... regretful. Worried about what we'd... done. I assured him it was fine, I'm clean, and it was just sex. Nothing major, and then I saw him at the fundraiser and—"

"You told him fucking him was no big deal?" she exclaimed.

Yes, because it wasn't...

But even as my thoughts wandered, as her tone hit me, I knew somehow it must have come across in a way I hadn't intended.

"Yes, because it's *not* a big deal. Sex is just... sex, Jamie. It doesn't mean we're fated mates like in those romance books you're always reading."

Jamie huffed, sighing deeply as she chose her words.

"You are such a dense asshole sometimes, but I guess I can't blame you. You haven't exactly dated many men with substance, so let me make this crystal clear for you, Wes."

My lips tightened along with my grip on my phone.

How dare she insult my choice in men! As if she is one to talk!

Before I could launch into a "that's the pot calling the kettle black" speech, Jamie's voice softened.

"Sex might not be a big deal to *you,* but it is to some of us. Some people don't give it up as easily as you do."

"Are you calling me a manwhore, Jamie?" I deadpanned.

"Yes, Weston. I am." She tutted.

She wasn't wrong. Not entirely anyway.

Perhaps that is part of the problem. I'm too detached.

But then again, in my life, attachments usually didn't pan out well for me. It wasn't like people hung around me for my intellect, or lack thereof apparently.

"I offered to buy him lunch, and he refused." I specifically left out the part where I hadn't *actually purchased* Cade lunch, but I did not need to feed Jamie any more ammo.

"Because it probably made him feel like shit. Like you were trying to pay him for—"

Oh.

Oh...

I closed my eyes as understanding befell me. I silently ran a hand over my face. This did not bode well for me.

I'd fucked up.

"Food and sex are not mutually exclusive..." I sighed defensively.

"You like him, don't you?" she said calmly.

How was it she always knew exactly what I didn't want to hear?

Her words made me feel strange. Vulnerable even.

Or maybe it's just the drinks I've had...

"I like what I know... of him." It was the truth. I didn't know him, not really. Not like I knew his favorite color or his shoe size, or who his parents were... but I knew he preferred Sam Adams, had an apparent love of Star Wars, and that he had a good heart. The man took care of animals, for God's sake. You can't love animals and be an asshole, it's just science.

"Beyond the spicy stuff?" Jamie asked hesitantly.

"He works for a veterinary hospital, and he's terrible at karaoke," I practically whispered in defeat.

Lord, take me now.

"Well, that doesn't sound like your type at all," she teased. Before I could speak, she cut in once more.

"If you really like this guy Weston, try... getting to *know* him. I know this might come as a shock to you, but *some* of us like it when a guy puts in some effort and doesn't just treat us like we're something that can be bought."

Effort.

I had certainly put in *effort*. I'd bought him a drink, offered to buy him lunch—which I'd come up short on thanks to my parents meddling as usual—and suddenly the image Cade must have formed of me hit me square in the head like a brick as Jamie's words settled in the air.

Perhaps, my current efforts had not been the brightest.

"Right. I could say the same to you, Jamie," I rebutted softly.

"I got to go, Wes. Dante is waiting for me inside," she said quietly before hanging up.

Just as we finished our call, the waiter stopped by with the check. The man smiled slyly at me, sliding the leather book toward me with a wink.

It was harrowing as I watched the man leave slowly, noticing the way in which he moved like a gazelle.

On any other given day, I would have let my gaze linger, but my conversation with Jamie had left me feeling a bit sour.

When I opened the book to glance at my check, I'd noticed the phone number scrawled at the bottom, and my heart sank.

Because for the first time in my too long single life, I felt different.

I ran my fingers over the ink, noting a bit smudged on my fingertips. It was fresh.

It would have been far too easy to leave a large tip, to catch this shimmering fish that was desperate to be hooked. It would have been no effort at all.

Make an effort.

Jamie's voice reverberated in my head.

I decided at that moment to leave a reasonable tip, sign the check, and get the hell out of Sedona.

What I wanted wasn't here, no.

What I wanted lay in Jasper Springs, and as I left Sedona, I barely registered as I walked past the waiter, and I did not meet his goodbye. Instead, I only focused on searching my social media for the Jasper Springs Pet Hospital, in search of a very big, sparkly fish.

CHAPTER SIXTEEN

Cade

I LEISURELY SIPPED my coffee as I sat down for breakfast at my kitchen island. I'd always been a stickler for my morning routine, and as such I did not usually check my messages or peruse my social media until I'd at least showered and dressed for the day.

As I took a bite of my cherry poptart, I noticed my Facebook messenger had a new message notification.

No one ever messaged me on the app, for most of the people I regularly saw or had contact with, knew I rarely checked the thing, and that texting my cell was a hell of a lot more efficient.

Still, I could not deny my budding curiosity, and so I opened the messenger, to see a message request that made my eyes widen.

Weston Rhodes would like to send you a message.

I stopped mid-chew to contemplate how I should respond, or *if* I should respond at all.

After all, Weston had said himself that just because we had sex, that didn't mean anything. And though he'd offered to grab us both something to eat, he hadn't shown up after. I knew I shouldn't have cared, after all, Weston was no different than the other assholes of my past, but I was still disappointed. A part of me had dared to *hope* that maybe, just maybe this once, things would be different.

But I also knew that it was rude to make assumptions.

So I did the noble, polite thing. I accepted the message.

I didn't know how else to get a hold of you. I wanted to apologize for... well... everything.

I feel like we got off on the wrong foot.

I glanced at Weston's profile picture, at his GQ smile and debonair attitude, at the little green circle that told me Weston was online. His pixelated face tempted me even then to answer.

And I couldn't deny him or his little icon as my fingers typed of their own accord.

You stood me up.

I chewed and swallowed the remainder of my poptart, feeling a sense of nervousness overcome me as I watched those three little dots flash on the screen.

I was detained. Believe me, I would have much rather been eating bon-bons with you.

I chewed my bottom lip as I considered his words.

Was there an emergency?

Cat stuck in a tree?

I actually felt a tad big smug at my cheeky response.

Score one for me!

Weston responded almost immediately.

Worse. My mother needed to parade me around like some prized pony.

Surprised at his candidness, I debated his words. He could be telling the truth, or it could be a lie, a cover up constructed to make him look better and not like an asshole, but...

But what reason would Weston have to lie to me?

What would he have to gain?

You catch more flies with honey than you do vinegar.

Against my better judgment, I tapped out a response, deciding to play with fire.

I see. Well, apology accepted. I guess.

I drank the last bit of my coffee as Weston typed out another message.

I don't feel like you've gotten the best impression of me, Cade. I think we should start over.

I cocked my head to the side as a smile threatened to erupt on my lips. It felt a little like he was groveling, and I had to admit, I kind of liked that idea.

Smooth, sexy Weston Rhodes on his knees begging for *me.*

Something about his words made me feel hopeful, emboldened.

And what exactly is the impression you think you gave me?

A pompous ass. Weston texted back.

My heartstrings tightened at the self-deprecation, and I was not sure what to say, but thankfully, Weston filled in the silence while I had my brain freeze.

Give me the chance to make it up to

you.

At that moment, I realized I'd gotten carried away, noting the time in the corner of my phone, which almost gave me a heart attack. I was ten minutes behind and should have already left for work by now.

Fuck!

I hurriedly got myself together, tapping out a response, hoping perhaps Weston would understand.

Sounds great, but I really have to go. I'm late for work.

CHAPTER SEVENTEEN

Cade

THE ENTIRE DRIVE to the pet hospital, I couldn't stop thinking about Weston and his somewhat endearing text.

Truthfully, I hadn't meant to sound so abrupt, and thought about texting him back, if only because I was now worried perhaps Weston hadn't gotten the best impression of *me*.

After all, I could admit maybe I'd been a bit forward at the bar, kissing Weston on stage, practically throwing myself at the man in the Uber, and running away after a panic attack... and then I'd brushed him off this morning, after he'd apologized.

Who's the asshole now?

The welcome sound of animals early in the morning would have deterred most, but after the last forty-eight hours, I was ready for some normalcy.

Except, once Diane shot around the corner, eyeing me up with those puppy dog eyes again, I knew I was surely doomed.

"Cade, I need you to—"

"Again?" I asked, not even bothering to hide my discomfort.

"I know it's a lot to ask, but I need someone reliable to head down to Rhodes Enterprises for the board meeting at two."

Say what now?

The name made me perk up with interest.

"What, uh... what for, exactly?" I asked as I ran a hand through my hair nervously.

"The board wants to go over last night's events, and get a plan going for the next two."

My entire body stiffened as her words hit me.

Two more events?

I was only aware of the one...

"I'm sorry, since when were there *three* events, total?" I asked, slightly panicked.

"It was always in the air, so we didn't want to get anyone's hopes up, but if the first event was successful, then Rhodes agreed to do two more across town. One in Paradise and one in Deer Park."

I breathed out a long sigh and nodded in understanding.

"So you want me to go down to Rhodes Enterprises and sell them on the idea of two more events."

Diane smiled, the sight lighting up the corners of her eyes and I knew I couldn't say no. Especially if the outcome meant more money and help for the hospital.

Maybe Weston would be there. Perhaps I could apologize for being so curt this morning.

What are the actual chances Weston will be there?

And even if he is, the place is probably huge. The chances are slim...

Still, I knew a slim chance was better than no chance at all, right?

"I mean, who can resist this face?" Diane said as she picked up the hospital's resident cat, Susie, snuggling her close. Susie had the audacity to look at me with her big, glossy kitten eyes, purring up a storm.

I pursed my lips, sighing in defeat.

Fine.

"When do I leave?" I deadpanned.

Diane smiled as Susie blinked her eyes shut. "The meeting is at two, so I suggest you leave after I come back from lunch at one."

I sighed, nodding as I checked the book for the day.

At least I'll get some time in doing my actual job.

CHAPTER EIGHTEEN

Cade

WHEN I ARRIVED at Rhodes Enterprises, I couldn't help but feel nervous.

The building stood out like a sore thumb, all sleek and shiny against the sunlight and greenery like an ominous, super-hero villain lair.

Does Batman work here too?

But if I was being honest with myself, it wasn't the building that had my stomach doing flips. It was the thought of seeing Weston, heir to the Bat Cave I stood in front of.

The inside of Rhodes Enterprises was just as shiny and futuristic, but then again, I would expect nothing less of a tech company like Rhodes.

"Can I help you?" an even, calm voice asked.

I turned to see a woman behind the lumbering metal desk, which was so shiny I could actually see my reflection in it.

"Um, yeah, actually... I, uh... I'm here from the Jasper Springs Pet Hospital," I said, clearing my throat, hoping to dredge up some confidence or semblance of bravado like Weston.

Instead, I chewed my lip as thoughts of the man pervaded me, of him in his sexy suit, latching his expensive watch and smiling that patented aristocratic smile men like him usually had.

The thoughts did nothing to quell my nervousness; in fact, they only made me long more for the man.

Focus, Cade!

"Wonderful, you can wait over there," she said as she pointed to an area equipped with white, egg-shaped chairs amidst a bright white floor and rug, floor to ceiling windows encasing the space and bathing it in bright light.

I am so out of my league, here.

I did as I was told, taking my seat in the strangely shaped chair, which swiveled without even a squeak.

What have I gotten myself into?

CHAPTER NINETEEN

Weston

I STROLLED THROUGH the halls of Rhodes Enterprises, feeling rather bored. For starters, there was nothing I loathed more than the drudgery of board meetings, which my father always *insisted* I join him for whenever I was in town on holiday.

It's like he's trying to bore me to death on purpose, perhaps to write me out of the will.

I casually pulled my phone out of my pocket, checking my messages for the hundredth time since that morning, to contemplate if I should respond back to Cade's abrupt exit text. He had agreed to a fresh start, but the last thing I wanted to do was appear... needy, or worse...

Clingy.

The fact I was worried about how I would come across to the golden-haired sexpot was baffling in itself, and should have been red flag *numero uno* to me. After all, I'd lived nearly thirty years not giving a shit what *anyone* thought of me. My parents, my coworkers, the newspapers or social media spies who liked to report my antics to embarrass me, my family, and the company.

So why did I care all of a sudden, about what the doe-eyed little cinnamon roll thought of me?

Why was making a *good impression* suddenly so important when it seemingly wasn't before?

"Morning, Mr. Rhodes," Cynthia, the desk attendant, called in her chipper, sing-song voice.

I barely looked up from my phone. But then again, I dealt with Cynthia just as much as I dealt with either of my parents. She was their right hand, after all.

"Morning, Cynthia. Where's this stupid meeting my father wants me at today?"

"Conference Room C on the fifth floor,"

she said sweetly, but I could see the disdain in her eyes when I finally looked up.

I knew how most of the people in the family business felt about me, which was just another reason why I wanted nothing to do with running my family's legacy, father's wishes or not.

How was I supposed to take over a company where no one even liked me because of their own preconceived notions?

Preconceived notions you helped feed with your drama, no doubt.

It was true, I had never set the record straight for any of them, not that it would have mattered. When people saw me, they saw the heir to Rhodes Enterprises, not the man who went home alone nearly every night to an empty penthouse with nothing but his hand and a stocked bar to keep him company.

They only saw the moments I wished would have lasted longer than a moment.

"Thank you, Cynthia," I murmured, trained in the art of thanking my father's assistant practically since my birth.

Sliding my phone back in my pocket, I pressed the elevator button, waiting impatiently so as to get this damn meeting over with. The sooner I showed up, played pretend for my father, the sooner I could go back to...

Was there anything truly worthwhile to go back to?

The realization struck me, cold and hard, in the chest like an icicle of truth. But I didn't want to think about cold, hard truths, and so I shoved the thoughts aside as the doors slid open, calling me forth like a lamb to the slaughter, and perhaps that was all this song and dance really was. I could fight and refuse all I wanted, but deep in my heart, I knew one day the inevitable would come.

As I sauntered down the crisp white and grey halls of the fifth floor, I noted how quiet it was, which only made the sound of my beating heart that much louder in my own ears.

And when I'd settled on Conference Room C, I'd opened the door expecting a boardroom full of company executives and my father.

But instead, what I found was something much, much better.

Cade.

"Well, well, look what the cat dragged

in," I purred, a smile forming on my face.

Cade's eyes widened in surprise, a blush creeping into his perfect, pale cheeks, and immediately my cock twitched at the sight, my pea brain throwing up images of Cade blushing before me... on his *knees.*

I let out a muffled sound as I shut the door, shifting my weight only slightly as to not draw attention to the sudden erection I'd sprung from the mere *sight* of the man.

"What are you doing here?" Cade asked, dumbfounded.

I couldn't help but widen my grin. "Well, I thought perhaps I'd be stomaching another grueling snoozefest of a meeting, but it appears today I'll be paying better attention," I said.

Cade's blush deepened as he swiveled back and forth in his chair.

"What exactly are *you* doing here, though? I did not peg you for the stalker type," I teased.

Cade blinked, just as he was about to answer me, the door behind us opened. Both of us turned to see a string of men in suits come piling in, filling the table rather quickly, followed by the latest concierge attendant, a woman I did not recognize, who had taken to passing out bottles of water as the suits took their seats.

All blushing and flirtation dissipated in the air as a familiar hand clapped my shoulder, tightening its grip. I'd know that touch anywhere.

"Morning, son," my father cooed, causing me to break my attention away from the man I would have much rather looked at.

"Morning, Dad."

"You're early. What a nice surprise."

"Yes, well, when there's nothing to do in this God-forsaken town except stare at the damn wall..." I sighed.

My father chuckled as he motioned for me to take a seat at the long oblong table.

"Well, some would call that *relaxing.*" he said as I took my seat. His smile was polite, but genuine.

Like a true proud papa.

"Nonetheless, the time for play has come to a close. We have business to attend to," my father's voice carried as he made his way to the front of the table, right next to Cade.

I watched as my father introduced himself, shaking Cade's hand. A surge of anxiety flooded me as I watched my father's carefully practiced business expression. I could not legitimately tell my father's impression of Cade and how he felt about him, a notion that should have been alarming to me.

I had never really sought my parent's approval, especially when it came to those I had relations with. I couldn't very well say I had ever introduced them to a serious boyfriend–not that I'd had one—or girlfriend, before I'd come out.

Not to mention, my coming out to my parents had not gone as smoothly as I had hoped. They were as supportive as wealthy, image obsessed parents could be, and they'd certainly "mellowed" out in the years since, but my father did not acknowledge my romantic liaisons at all to this day, while my mother only really let her opinions be known after a drink or two.

Or four.

Still, the burgeoning need to hear their praise was an ember that would not die inside of my scorched soul, no matter how many men I seduced.

I watched like a fly on the wall as my father, and some of the other suits, addressed Cade, asking him questions about the hospital, about how much money they'd raised at the event, and their history with fundraising in general.

Cade fired off answers confidently, like a true natural. It was more than apparent that on this particular topic, that of animal care and veterinary science, Cade was in his element, and I couldn't help but stare in awe.

While the man seemed mild-mannered and quiet at first glance, below the pretty blue eyes and California surfer hair, he was a force all his own, whether he knew it or not. He was more than just attractive. He was passionate, smart, and caring.

He's such a good person.

Like sunshine in a bottle.

So fucking good.

I couldn't help but let my thoughts wander to just how I'd like to praise him for doing such a good job selling the pitch.

The image of Cade on his knees in the board room, my fingers threaded through his hair as his cheeks hollowed while he sucked me off pushed to the forefront of my mind, and I had to bite my knuckle to keep from groaning with pleasure at the thought.

Almost as if he could sense my inner turmoil, he turned his bright blue peepers at me for just a second, causing my heart to beat faster.

The image of Cade spread across the conference room table as I filled him caught like wildfire in my brain, causing the blood to rush to my cheeks as well as my cock, and I nonchalantly palmed my throbbing cock beneath the table, adjusting myself once more.

Cade looked away, smiling genuinely at my father and nodding in agreement to whatever the hell he'd just said.

Now is not the time!

"I think we have all the information we need, Mr. Green, thank you. We'll be in touch," my father said, and I realized the meeting was over.

I hadn't really gathered a word they said, my attention focused on keeping myself steady and stable in front of my father's employees and the man who seemed to have me entirely second-guessing everything in my life.

As they said their goodbyes, shaking hands and being polite, I realized at any moment Cade would walk through the door, and I could not let him do so without at least telling him he had done so well.

And then perhaps, all praise aside, I could take the good boy out for a well-deserved and overdue lunch.

"I'll be out in a minute," I said, smiling half-heartedly at my father, who nodded in response on his way out.

When the last of the suits had gone, Cade made his way to the door, but I casually shut it, stepping in front of his exit.

"Ah, ah. Not yet. We have some more *business* to discuss," I purred smoothly.

To my surprise, Cade cocked an eyebrow at me, crossing his arms in a way that was most enticing.

"And what business might that be?" he asked sarcastically, but I did not miss the hint of a smile tugging at his lips.

Oh, you want to play, do you?

Good thing for you, I love to play...

"Well, as good businessmen do, and quite often, I may add—" I licked my lips, continuing my suave speech. "I believe we should discuss *our private business* over lunch."

"Mhmmm."

"You did very well, up there," I said as I took a step closer to him.

Cade's blue eyes gazed up at me with interest.

"You flatter me, Weston, but all I did was just... read numbers and figures. That's it. A monkey could have done it. I hardly think that's a job well done."

I stopped just in front of him, sliding my hands in my pockets, adjusting my unruly erection and to prevent me from wrapping my arms around this man and telling him what I really thought of his performance.

Or rather, what performance I *wished* I could see of him in this stuffy boardroom.

Make an effort, Wes.

Beyond the physical.

"I do owe you a lunch. After I... how did you say it? Stood you up?"

Cade leaned into my space just a fraction, close enough I could smell his sweet, intoxicating scent.

Cinnamon and cloves mixed with cedar and orange... delicious.

"Mhmm. I suppose you *do* deserve the chance to make a better... impression," he said as he looked up at me from under his lashes.

Cade was playing with me, and I wanted nothing more than to take his bait. I could not help but smile, even though my insides were clamoring with excitement.

"And I promise you, *Cade*, I will not disappoint you again."

Cade's eyes lit up with amusement as I breathed his name.

"Dear lord, I hope not," he said as he swallowed nervously, his gaze dipping to my lips for a moment, that welcome tinge of pink coloring his cheeks again.

"Do you have something you desire, Cade? Something that will please your palette?" I asked, my heartbeat in my throat. It would be so very easy for me to close the gap between us, for me to run my hands through Cade's silky locks and covet his mouth to sing him my praise.

But I wanted *more*.

I wanted more than a quick, steamy, forbidden kiss in my father's boardroom. Make no mistake, I still wanted those things, but there was something I wanted more.

I wanted a date.

With Prince Charming.

A real, honest to God date in which I could bask in Cade's golden glow for longer than a moment, hear him laugh, and listen to him wail on about the drudgery of every day life in Jasper fucking Springs.

What has happened to me?

"Um... Bernard's is good, I guess," he breathed the name of the cafe so huskily, I had to stifle another petulant moan of my own.

I want to hear him breathe my name like that.

"I could go for something quite robust myself, right about now," I said as I caught his cerulean gaze.

"I need to make a stop first, but, uh... I'll meet you there?" he said as he moved past me for the door.

I moved instinctively, giving him the out he needed. Despite my desire to keep him locked up in here forever with me, I knew I couldn't do so. I glanced at my watch, noting the time. It was barely two thirty.

"I will be there at three thirty," I noted as I moved away, regaining my composure as I opened the door for Cade.

"See you then," Cade said as he

blushed once more, exiting the building, leaving me feeling quite excited for once.

This day was turning out to be better than I'd thought.

CHAPTER TWENTY

Cade

WHEN I FINALLY made it to the sanctity of my car, I had to catch my breath. Not because the walk from the fifth floor to the lobby had been brisk, but because I was rather certain that if I hadn't left when I did, I would have kissed Weston.

Again.

What the hell is wrong with me?

I'm not usually like this!

It was like every time I got near the man, I became some wanton, needy thing. The smell of his cologne, the darkness in his gem-like eyes that called to me like a moth to a flame. The way his voice was smooth like melted chocolate and caused my stomach to flip, my cock to twitch. On the physical end of things... he was absolutely perfect. It was like he was crafted from my love of rom-coms and my darkest fantasies or something.

Weston Rhodes seemed to bring out parts of myself I'd never known existed until I met him.

And seeing him swivel back and forth in his chair, amidst the crystal chandelier and stark, sleek design of the Rhodes Enterprises conference room, only hammered it into my skull that Weston was cut from a finer cloth. Despite knowing he was out of my league, I still wanted to wrap myself in that smooth, sexy cloth.

I turned the car on, the air conditioning blasting against my warm skin as I opened my phone, dialing the number of the one person who could talk me down from a burgeoning panic attack.

"Everything okay?" Dawson asked, his voice only slightly alarmed. It wasn't as if I called him regularly. Usually, I'd shoot him a text, but I could not do such a thing when my mind was rushing a thousand miles a minute.

"I have a date. With Weston."

Dawson whistled on the other end of the phone, the cool air from the vents blowing on my face.

"Well, I'll be damned," he said with a chuckle.

"I'm freaking out," I said, hearing my voice shake a little.

"Why? It's just a date. It's not like you're marrying the guy."

"Because he's... him... and I'm... me, and you know my social skills are sorely lacking and, like, what will we even talk about? I have nothing interesting to say or—"

"Pump the brakes, Cade. Breathe. Take a deep breath, and just *breathe,* buddy."

Immediately, Dawson shifted from his cavalier, charismatic air to firefighter mode, the one where he was serious and tackled everything with stoic poise and grace; the one he reserved for settling down fights or holding it together to pull someone from a burning building.

Dawson was mostly an aloof, overconfident pain in the ass, but when push came to shove, he was the best man to be in anyone's corner. It also helped that he at least had dealt with my anxiety before, both on a friendly and not-so friendly level.

I did as he instructed, sucking in a deep breath as we counted to ten.

"You've been on dates before. It's not something you don't know how to do. And I can honestly tell you, your conversation skills are fine. Just be yourself."

I let out a dark, strangled laugh. "You mean the anxious, self-deprecating, shut-in who lives on rom-coms and ice cream?"

Dawson sighed. "You forgot the bunny slippers, but no. I mean the successful man who doesn't seem to know he's a fucking catch. You bought your own damn house, Cade. You are amazing at your job, you're bomb at karaoke, I don't care what you say, you make a mean risotto, and on a scale of one to ten, you are a fucking twenty. Don't sell yourself so short."

Dawson's words hit me like a ton of bricks. Even when we'd been together, he'd never talked to me like that. It wasn't jealousy or remorse, but rather a cold, hard truth. Dawson laid it out, and for the first time, I had the inkling to believe him.

"I guess I don't normally see myself the

way you see me."

"It's not just me, Cade. Everyone who knows you, knows you deserve more than the bullshit you *think* you deserve. You're a fucking gem. So go be a *gem*. Go on the date, smile and be yourself. Have a good time. I guarantee you, that's all you'll need. The rest will fall into place, and you'll have that guy eating out of your palm in no time."

I turned to look at the looming building of Rhodes Enterprises, feeling a little better.

It's just a date. It's not forever.

And I am starving.

"Thanks, Dawson," I said as my nerves started to settle.

"Anytime, buddy," he said, his tone going soft before he hung up.

I took another deep breath and counted to ten, then drove off in the direction of Bernard's.

CHAPTER TWENTY-ONE

Cade

I WALKED THROUGH the front door of Bernard's with one goal—to give Weston *my* best impression. And also to have fun and get a damn whiskey barbecue burger with a side of extra fries because I was starving.

I'd called Diane to tell her I'd be coming back a little late, on account that I was having lunch with one of the 'employees' of Rhodes Enterprises, as was customary for business. It wasn't a *complete* lie, Weston had assured me such luncheons were a normal thing between business partners, and as far as she knew, we were partners.

I just wasn't sure if it was business or pleasure, or perhaps both.

Maybe if things go well, Weston and I will see each other again... at the next event.

I spotted Weston before the hostess looked up from her phone. He sat off to the left of the restaurant, which at this hour during the week, the restaurant itself was practically deader that a doornail.

Still, in the midst of the place, Weston looked refined in his suit, his watch glinting in the amber light to really drive home his apparent Bruce Wayne look.

Almost instantly he caught my gaze, rising to wave me over.

You got this, Cade.

I pulled up a seat across from him as the waiter came by to take our drink orders.

"I'll have a scotch on the rocks, and my friend here will have a—" He looked at me in question for a moment, and it dawned on me he was giving me a choice.

"Ice tea with lemon, please," I said politely.

"Any appetizers for you guys, or do you

need a few more minutes?" the waiter asked.

"I'd love some of your famous buffalo chicken dip," Weston said with a smile, and I had to admit I was a little surprised. I didn't exactly peg him for a buffalo chicken guy. Then again, I didn't really know him beyond the flesh, and what little interactions we had had.

Which made me feel like an asshole for assuming. Nevertheless, I pushed the melancholy aside in favor of turning a new leaf, just as Weston had.

When the waiter walked away, it was just the two of us facing off against one another.

"I worried you might have changed your mind," Weston said as he leaned back in his chair, his long, lithe fingers tapping gently on the starched linen tablecloth.

"Well, you did say you owe me, so it would be rude to refuse you a chance to how did you say it? Make a better impression?" I said as I leaned back in my chair, shooting him a smile of my own.

"That I do," he said with a grin as the waiter brought our drinks and a large bowl of buffalo chicken dip with fresh made tortilla chips.

"So are you in town long, or..."

Weston shook his head. "I came because my father *insisted* I see him and the company doing something other than what they are known for. He thinks if he shows me *all the aspects* of this business, something will take and I'll just want to up and move here tomorrow to take over."

"Is that something you want?" I ask, making polite conversation.

So far so good.

Weston's eyes dimmed, as he twisted his lips, pausing before answering.

"It's what is expected of me. I am the heir to the business. What I want doesn't factor into the equation," he said as he immediately dove in for a chip, absolutely avoiding the path this conversation was headed on. I watched as he scooped up a heaping amount of dip and I couldn't help but let out a small laugh. Mid-chew he looked at me, raising an eyebrow. I had to admit, it was a sound tactic for evading an uncomfortable discussion.

Like I've never tried to talk about something other than work before.

"What?" he said through half a mouthful of food.

"Oh nothing, its just, uh... you have a little something," I said pointing to the corner of my own mouth.

Weston's deep green eyes lit up with mischief as he swallowed his chip and dip, his tongue flicking out to lick the splash of hot sauce there. The sight alone made my cock twitch, and I cleared my throat. Weston only grinned slyly.

The waiter came back, and I half wondered if he was just rushing back to make my life that much more drawn out, or if he was just keeping his normal pace and I was the one who was antsy.

"We're still going to need a few minutes," Weston touted, before looking at me. "Unless of course, you already know what you'd like?"

His words made my stomach flip, as the look in his eyes told me he most certainly wasn't talking about food.

Two can play this game, Mr. Rhodes.

"Actually," I said as I leaned forward in my chair, stretching my arm out across the table on the opposite side of him, tapping my fingernails on the tablecloth, channeling my best Weston impression.

"I will have the whiskey barbecue cheeseburger with extra pickles and sauce, and extra fries on the side," I said, dropping my voice an octave, mimicking the smoothness of Weston's natural tone.

Weston looked a little surprised, but he hid it well. Clearly he wanted to play the big, hot alpha suit who gets to order for their sweet and subby darling, but I was feeling somewhat emboldened by Dawson's words, and my little white lie to my boss. I was breaking the rules today, and perhaps the bad boy fever was driving me over the edge.

Bad boys usually get punished after all.

Weston shrugged.

"I'll have what he's having," he said with a wink, and the waiter gathered our menus before toddling off in the direction of the kitchen, leaving us to our own devices.

Weston shook his head, his dark hair swaying from the motion as he breathed a contented sigh.

"You're refreshing, do you know that?" he said as he took a sip of his scotch, straightening the wrinkles in his button-down once more.

The sight made little flashes pop up in my memory, of just how I'd watched those fingers slide over the miniscule wrinkles, over his taut chest... shirt soaked in sweat.

I shifted in my seat, my cock jumping at the memory.

"I don't see how. You aren't the only one who's given a doozy of a first impression," I say honestly, dispelling my momentary Weston impression.

"I don't know what you mean," he said as he dug for another chip, this time taking a little less of a giant heap of the dip.

"I mean, I know I kind of came off... abrupt the other morning, maybe even a little standoffish. Then at the fundraiser... I... I just wasn't myself. I was kind of... stressed."

Weston took a sip of his scotch before speaking.

"Would that stress have anything to do with my... reassurances?"

It was now my turn to dive into the dip and hide my words.

"You were a little... cold."

"You seemed worried about what had happened. Remorseful. I only wanted to assure you that if it meant nothing to you..." His words disappeared as his gaze dipped to where my hand still lay, fingers curled into a fist not far from him.

Understanding befell me as I realized all at once what he meant.

"If it meant nothing to me, you wanted to reflect that."

"Stage five clinger is not a good look for me, Cade," he said as he shoved a chip in his mouth.

"I know the feeling. All my exes used to say I was too needy," I breathed, instantly regretting the moment the words left my mouth.

Why the fuck would I say that?

Even if it was true, that's like date etiquette 101! Never talk about your exes!

Weston laid his free hand on the table, fingers curled into a fist only a hair's breadth away from mine.

"I wish I could be, though. Needy. Clingy. Affectionate. But most of my affections have come with a price tag, because *that* is how my exes preferred it. They didn't want my feelings, either."

The admittance makes my heart break for this man. Weston didn't move his hand, instead he stared at it, looked at the space between us with anticipation, longing.

I slowly uncurled my fingers, which

put my pinky only an inch away from his wrist.

The desire to touch him, to soothe *his* worries, to *reassure* him was so strong, it was practically magnetic.

And suddenly all the nerves I had before went up in smoke as I slid my hand closer, next to his, our skin brushing in the lightest of ways.

Teasing, asking for permission.

"Kinda sounds like you dated some assholes," I said.

Weston jumped a little from the contact, but eased up nearly instantly. His green eyes gazed back at me with a depth I'd never seen in anyone else before.

"You sound like you have experience with that," he said softly.

I felt rather on the spot at his statement, but for the first time in my life, it felt like a weight had been taken off my shoulders at the same time.

The truth for once felt... freeing. Dawson was right.

I'd gone after assholes because I thought it was what I deserved, and that truth helped me see the recognition in Weston's eyes.

He thought he deserved them too, but

it was clear to me as he fought to give in to his obvious desire, that maybe he deserved more too.

He'd just never asked for it.

"Yeah, you could say that."

At that moment, the waiter decided to bring our cheeseburgers, and Weston pulled his hand back, leaving mine alone.

The strange air of vulnerability had broken, as Weston shook his head, dispelling all thoughts and confessions for the moment in favor of sweet, sticky barbecue sauce and bacon grease.

I watched as he bit into his burger, his eyes practically rolling back in his head.

"Oh fuck, Cade..." he moaned, making my cock throb.

I want to hear him say those words about me...

I cleared my throat. "Uh..."

"This is the best burger I think I've ever had," he said as some barbecue sauce dripped down his chin.

I smirked before picking up my own and diving in. The salty sweetness on my tongue was divine, and I was pretty hungry.

"You ain't kidding," I said with a light laugh as I took another bite, practically devouring my burger in a matter of seconds.

The rest of the lunch was like that. The two of us completely annihilating our sandwiches, laughing, talking about stupid shit.

Like weird food combinations, movie recommendations. What the secret ingredient was in Sandra's homemade pralines.

Weston insisted it was espresso powder, but I didn't believe him.

By the time the check had come, I was a little shocked. Though it had been an hour, it felt like time had just flown by way too fast.

I liked talking to him.

Hell, I liked *him.*

I knew it was crazy after one lunch to think you knew someone, but I was starting to know Weston Rhodes.

Not the Weston that I'd seen in articles on the Internet, or the one who swiveled around sexily in his egg chair at Rhodes Enterprises.

But the one who knew all the words to *Don't Go Breaking My Heart,* understood my Star Wars reference, apparently had an obsession with buffalo chicken dip, and who fought me tooth and nail to pay the bill.

"At least let me pitch in," I whined.

Weston shook his head. "Absolutely not. I owe you."

I watched him sign the check and hand it off hastily. I sighed, my shoulders relaxing as I arose from my chair.

"Well, since you insisted. Thank you. But you should let me return the favor... sometime," I said as Weston came behind me, setting his hand against the small of my back. He gently touched me, pushing me toward the doors. I walked slowly, never moving to remove his hand. I liked how it felt, warm against my shirt.

Calming, soothing.

When we exited Bernard's the sun warmed my air-conditioned blood.

I turned to look at him, if only to say thank you again, make my exit. But I stopped frozen underneath his gem-like gaze, my gaze dipping to his pouty, perfect lips. I noticed a smidge of barbecue sauce in the corner of his mouth, and the innate desire in me to *lick* it off of him made me realize I was truly in over my head.

As if he could sense my sudden

inkling, he reached out to brush some of my hair behind my ear, his voice dropping an octave.

"I think I'd like that, Cade," he said softly.

Instinctively, I leaned into him, against his chest. Suddenly, I felt dizzy and I knew it wasn't from the lunch or the sun.

Weston moved closer, his free hand settling at my hip, his palm warm against me.

I looked up at him for a moment, readying myself for what felt like the most right thing in the world.

Weston licked his lips, his eyes searching mine.

My eyelids fluttered, and I leaned in just an inch, expecting him to meet me halfway.

To kiss me like they do in the movies.

His fingers gripped my hair as he brought his forehead to mine, letting out a sigh.

"I had a really great time today, Cade. With you," he whispered.

"Same," I whispered back.

"But all good things must come to an end, and we must return to our dreadful nemesis. Employment."

At that moment, I realized he wasn't going to kiss me.

And why should he?

It was a date, and we had fun, but...

He was right. The real world beckoned us, popping our perfect little Bernard's Bubble.

"Right," I said as I licked my lips, nodding in understanding.

"Will, uh... talk later?" I asked, feeling the nerves starting to kick up again.

Weston slid his fingers down my jaw, resting his hand on my collarbone. He implored me with deep, sorrowful eyes.

"Absolutely," he said as he slid his hand off my neck, turning away and heading for a car that I realized had been sitting in front of us since we'd exited.

Must be his driver.

I watched as Weston languidly folded himself into the backseat, as he closed the door and sped off.

I'd wanted him to kiss me. To sweep me off my small town feet and whisk me away to his Christmas Tree farm or Italian Villa or whatever it is that men like him had in those cheesy movies.

But that wasn't the realization that shocked me, no.

I was always the one who wished to be kissed, to be swept off their feet.

But in that moment, before he set his hand on my hip, before he tugged me closer, I realized I wanted to kiss *him.*

I wanted to crush my lips to his and bring him into me tenfold, wrap my arms around him and soothe his tired, achy heart.

I wanted to be *his* prince charming, come to save *him* from all the assholes.

And I'd missed my chance.

Hopefully, I'll get the chance to make it up to him.

CHAPTER TWENTY-TWO

Weston

IF THERE WAS one thing I hated more than coming home, it was dinner with my parents. I knew how much of a dick that made me sound like, but I didn't care. No one could really understand the whole vibe of the Rhodes when they were off the clock.

But despite my own personal feelings of being subjected to parental gaslighting, I knew it would be easier to just play along and get it over with.

Sit down with mom and dad, have some dinner, listen to their nitpicking and take it with a smile. Dad would give the usual 'one day when I'm gone' speech, and I could make my exit after that.

So, when I pulled up to the Rhodes house, I was already in a shit mood and I didn't anticipate a sunny, cheery dinner.

Not to mention I was still kicking myself for not leaning in and kissing Cade when it was more than apparent that was what he wanted.

What is happening to me?

I exited my Uber, the melancholy settling in as I looked up the long driveway at the colonial style mansion that I spent most of my summers in and out of. The dogwood trees framing the yard and the stark, white columns in the front of the house looked ominous. Walking through the front door was like walking through the gates of heaven, or hell, if you actually knew what lay behind them.

"Oh, hello Weston," my mother said cheerily as I opened the door. She stood in the foyer with a martini in her hand, her cheeks rosy and her eyes bright. Judging by the cavalier way she pulled me into a hug, practically sloshing her gin, I would have bet it was at least the third she'd had. *It's happy hour somewhere, dear,* she'd always say.

"Mother," I said dryly as I set my hand on her back lightly, steadying her for the moment.

"You are early, again," my father said as he came down the hall, scotch in hand, sleeves rolled up to his elbows.

His immediate presence made me straighten my stance, made whatever miniscule feelings of contentedness I had felt disappear in the cold, bitter air of the foyer.

"Father," I said as I let go of my mother.

The scent of roast duck hit me, along with the pungent smell of garlic and I had to work to keep my face even. I never cared for the fowl, no matter how they prepared it.

Mother waved her hand, dismissing my father. "No matter what time he shows up, dear. This is his *home*."

Yup, definitely her third.

"Home is in the city, mother, but thanks."

My father's eyes met mine for a moment, a dark look passing through his. It was as if he wanted to say something, but he refused.

Odd, usually the man just says what

he wants with no regard to how other people will take it.

"Pish posh, darling, you will always be a Rhodes and therefore all roads will eventually lead you *home* to Jasper Springs where you belong."

I dismissed her comment as she toddled off toward the kitchen. My father followed her without question, brushing past me with an intensity that made me feel on edge.

I'd rather he just say his piece and get on with it, so I could get on with my damn life.

I followed my parents through the oversized kitchen, past the actual chef, since my mother never touched a stove in her life, and the only time she used a cutting board was to slice her lemons and limes for her cocktails.

"Smells delicious, Margo," I said with a rueful smile as I passed by.

Margo, who'd been the family chef since I was about eight, only looked at me with a bright smile of her own and a warmth that actually settled my nerves some.

"Thank you, sir," she said sweetly.

I hated it when people did that. Called

me *sir* like I was some old man, at least in the presence of my every day life.

However, I certainly didn't mind it one bit when a blue-eyed god with silky blond hair and the lips of a fucking angel called me sir. Or submitted to my commands.

That I could get used to.

The thoughts of Cade pervaded my senses again, and I let out a defeated sigh. Now was really not the time, but I couldn't help but feel guilty. The lunch had gone... well.

Too well, if I was being honest.

I found myself opening up to Cade in a way I hadn't really opened up to anyone else before. Something about his demeanor, his presence, just made me loose-lipped. It was like I could tell him *anything.*

And when he'd gotten all dominant for the blip of a moment, shooting me that dead-sexy look as he dropped the tone of his voice, I saw the undeniable monster inside of Cade begging to come out, and I...

Liked it.

I liked it a whole fucking lot.

Reel me in, sir, I am yours.

I could only hope I hadn't completely

botched my chances with the man because I didn't take the obvious opening.

The heat and attraction that existed between Cade and I was obvious, but Jamie's words clung to me like a bad rash.

Make an effort.

So that's what I did. I made the effort. I evaded kissing Cade because I knew if I kissed him, I'd fall into my old patterns. I'd wrap him up in my tentacles once more and covet him all to myself, and we'd wind up in the same place we had that night after karaoke.

And for the first time in my life, I had to admit that I wanted more than just to shove my cock down Cade's throat.

I wanted to see him again. I wanted to see him as much as I could while I was here in town.

I took my seat at the long, ornate dining table that looked like it was set for a party, despite the fact there was only the three of us. The manners that were forever ingrained in me were involuntary. I placed the napkin on my lap, reached for my glass of cold, freshly poured Icelandic water, whilst Margo set about to serving us.

"So about the meeting this afternoon..."

My father's words elicited a sigh from me and a curse from my mother, as he gingerly picked up his fork. He didn't even look at me as he said it.

"For fuck's sake, can we just enjoy a nice dinner with our son without discussing business?" my mother bit out before shaking her empty martini glass in the air.

Margo swiped it with precision, trained well in my mother's routine.

"This is a family matter, and therefore it should be discussed over family dinner," my dad touted, dismissive as usual.

I rolled my eyes as Margo refilled my mother's glass, the heavy scent of garlic making my eyes water.

"Well, I'd have to say I think this is a new record. I've barely been here fifteen minutes and you're already up my ass," I said as Margo set down a glass of home brewed tea for me. I looked up at her for a moment, taking in her kind smile. I nodded in thanks, gracious for the gesture. She'd even put two slices of lemon in it, just the way I liked. I took a strong sip as my father guffawed.

"I wouldn't have to lay into you, Weston, if you actually entertained this conversation and accepted things. But with as little as we see you, a man has to take the chances he's given."

"Gee, it's almost like I don't come around because of this very issue," I growled as I set to cutting into my tender duck breast, probably slicing a little too enthusiastically.

My mother groaned, taking a sip of her martini. "I just wanted a nice family dinner..." she complained.

"I don't understand why you are so resistant to this. The company is doing well, and you would do well to have some stability in your life. Put roots down, build a life, a—"

"I'm glad you think the life *I built* in the city isn't a life. I'll take that one to my therapist. I'm sure we can squeeze a few pricey sessions out of that," I snarked back.

Truth was I had no therapist, but he didn't need to know that.

"You haven't had a job in over a year, Weston, and I've never seen you seriously entertain finding *someone* to settle down with. All you do is mope around that damn condo and stay out till all hours of the morning doing God knows what with God knows who..." My father's face flushed with pink, his eyes getting glassy.

I hadn't seen him this worked up since I came out of the closet. I fought to look away, but it was like watching a damn train wreck. I just couldn't help myself.

"It might not be the life *you* wanted for me, dad but it is *my* life."

"Your life is here, Weston. With this company, with your family!" he yelled.

My mother sobbed into her martini glass.

"My life is with whoever I want it to be, wherever the fuck I want to be!" I yelled back as I threw my napkin down, rising from my seat. I'd had enough of this.

"I think I've lost my appetite," I said as I stormed out of the dining room, my father's angry voice bellowing beside me.

"One day you'll have to grow up and be a fucking adult, Weston!"

His words hit me like a gong. The vibration sounded through every bone, every blood-filled vein in my body.

Walking away from a situation that brought me no peace was about the most adult thing I could think of.

And sure, before I'd come to Jasper Springs, before I met *Cade*, I would have risen to his bait. I would have bit back and yelled, and stirred the shit pot some more, but I was too tired to deal with it all that day.

So instead, I said nothing. I gave my father my back and walked out of the house, down the driveway feeling nothing but rage and frustration, and shame.

I'd never be what they wanted.

What my father wanted.

No amount of sitting in boardrooms and taking pictures would ever make me the businessman he wanted me to be.

I kept my pace quick as I turned down the road. I needed to clear my head of all this nonsense, this bullshit that my family loved to dig up every time I saw them.

I'd entertained the idea once. When I was seventeen.

I had come home from boarding school that summer, and I agreed to volunteer at the company, thinking I was going to be *in* those board meetings, helping to make decisions about the business. But instead, my father had assigned me to gopher status. Getting coffees, delivering lunches and mail, sending company emails and sorting paperwork.

Grunt work.

I'd expressed an interest, and my father treated me like it was Take Your Kid To Work day, telling me, "Everyone starts at the bottom, son."

I quickly realized that if I was going to be stuck on the bottom of the Rhodes food chain, perhaps I didn't have the stomach or drive to build myself up to the high standards my father had obviously set for me.

That was the summer I realized maybe there were *other* options for me.

Options that didn't include working for my asshole father.

So I withdrew from the company, left home early and couch-surfed on my sort of gay fuck-buddy from school's couch until the semester started. I'd made it my goal to stay as far away from Jasper Springs and Rhodes Enterprises since.

Step by step, I walked at high pace, relishing in the air against my heated skin, my emotions flourishing through me with every stride. Stuck in my head, I didn't even see the man I'd crashed into, nearly taking us both down on the sidewalk in front of...

The Jasper Springs Pet Hospital.

Shit, how long have I been walking?

Warm palms steadied my arms, and a familiar voice pulled me from my dark thoughts.

"Wes, are you... okay?" Cade's voice was like the sound of angels singing, soothing something in my tortured soul.

I eased in his grip as we both stood straighter, my heart catching in my throat. I looked down at him, into his pretty blue eyes. They reminded me of the ocean at night, when the waves calmly crash against the sand, smoothing the rough bits out and turning it to something softer, more pliable. Capable of building great sandcastles.

"I, uh... just needed to clear my head. Maybe, uh... grab a drink somewhere."

I cleared my throat, every ounce of my being wanted to close the gap between us.

I wanted to hide away in Cade Green's kiss, in his arms, until the sun came up and took away all this bullshit with it.

Cade seemed to understand my thoughts, like the mind reader he was.

"Okay, well, there's always M's Place..."

he said carefully.

"You, uh... want to get a drink... with me?" I asked hopefully.

Cade's eyes furrowed for a moment, his lips pursing as he let out his own breath. He nodded.

"Sure. Come on, I'll drive," he said as he nodded in the direction of the parking lot. The only car left at this hour was his, and a part of me felt nervous.

It wasn't like I'd never been in a car with another man before. Hell, I've had sex in the backseat of more cars than I can probably count on one hand.

But something about letting Cade take the proverbial wheel, following him into the tiny, personal space, was both intriguing and scary.

But I did it anyway, because I've always been hell for consequences.

Live in the moment was kind of my motto.

So as Cade opened the passenger door for me, as I folded myself into his tiny little white Civic, that was what I focused on.

Cade, my prince charming with a white steed.

CHAPTER TWENTY-THREE

Weston

AFTER THE SECOND scotch, I started to feel a little better, the edge finally taken off.

Cade leaned against the high-top table, taking a pull of his beer. He'd been nursing the one all evening, which I guess, I could ascertain why. The last time we were both here, we'd gotten sloppy drunk and ended up fucking.

Something that was clearly out of the norm for Cade, though I couldn't deny the experience hadn't been a bad one, but...

I wanted him to feel comfortable. Not just here in this bar, but... with me.

I wanted him to trust me, to *like* me... and not just the me that everyone else gets.

The real me.

The fucked up, hot mess that absolutely doesn't have his shit together and has more issues than Vogue.

I wanted someone to see my disaster and not turn away.

"So... do you want to talk about it, or..."

"My dad is a grade A dick," I said, feeling that incessant word-vomit I got around Cade rearing its ugly head.

"He wants me to take over the company, settle down. *Build a life here.*" I scoff as I took a sip of my scotch.

Cade's gaze didn't wander one bit, just stayed fixed on me like he was studying a leopard in its natural habitat or something.

It dawned on me, when he didn't speak, he was waiting for me to continue, so I did.

"I guess, I just... wish he understood that my life is what *I* make it, you know?"

Cade nodded.

"Yeah, I do know actually. I, uh... I might not have a dick dad with big expectations, but, um... I've always wanted to be the main character in my own life. I built everything I have on my own. I wanted this white picket fence life, like the ones in the movies... because a lot of people told me I couldn't. Because I was..."

He didn't have to say it. I knew exactly what he meant. People are always going to make assumptions of you, gay, straight, pan, bi, ace... and those assumptions and limitations can wear you down or they can give you the best drive, the best revenge. The need to say *I told you so* can be a great motivator in life for some people, and I guess I'd subscribed to it myself. I understood Cade with the utmost sympathy and empathy.

It's hard enough *being* gay on a good day, let alone when you have no support from others around you, when you already feel isolated and lonely.

"I made it my goal to have the house with the white picket fence and a perfect job with wonderful coworkers," he said, his lips turning up into a smile.

It was clear he did love his job, a sentiment I couldn't relate to. I'd never loved any job I'd been at, but I came close at Men's Warehouse. I did genuinely enjoy fitting people for suits and talking fashion. My coworkers were awesome too.

The sparkle in his eyes dissolved as he continued though, but he didn't look at me. Rather, he gripped his beer, picking at the waterlogged label.

"But I'm still coming up short," he said.

I frowned.

"How so?" I asked, feeling the innate desire to soothe his troubles like he did for me.

"Because none of it matters if I don't have anyone to share it *with*," he said, his voice cracking.

I didn't think twice about setting my hand on his, as his words struck a chord within my damn soul.

I didn't have anyone to share my life with either. Every time I thought I had found someone, someone *good*, they turned out to be just as selfish and materialistic as the person before. Lording things over me to get what they wanted, peacing out when they'd had their fill of cock and expensive gifts.

When the next Sugar Daddy came along with gifts far better than mine.

More than anything I'd wanted the very same thing Cade did.

Someone to go to the French Riviera with on holiday, who I could come home and curl up on the couch with to Netflix and chill, who I could bake fucking cookies with during a snowstorm and fuck senseless till the wee hours of the morning.

Someone to wake up with and have breakfast, who wouldn't walk out on me when the energy of the moment wore off.

Cade looked at my hand and then at me. His cheeks reddened a bit, his lips betraying him, showing the ghost of a smile on his face.

Why does he hold back?

I asked myself this, wondering if I was holding back too.

"Some things are just better with another person," I said, feeling my heart in my throat.

Cade swallowed, flipping his hand so that our fingers intertwined. He studied the sight for a moment, before nodding in agreement.

"I suppose they are," he said before letting go.

"I should, uh, we should probably

head out soon. The presentation must have gone well, because my boss told me we're to set up for another fundraiser tomorrow over in Deer Park around noon, so..."

My eyes widened a bit.

That was fast... my father must have really liked Cade's presentation, and the event must have made a decent amount for him to consider moving so quickly.

Suddenly, I feel a sting of guilt. Maybe that's what he wanted to discuss. The fundraiser. I'd been at the last one, and it only made sense, that if I was home under his watchful forced eye to learn about the philanthropic side of the business, he'd want me at the next one.

But if I'd stayed in that house I surely would have popped my cap, and I certainly wouldn't have run into Cade...

Instinctively, I pulled my phone out of my pocket, readying to que up a driver, but Cade reached out, his hand blocking my screen as he pushed it down. I looked up, to meet his gaze, full of empathy and something else.

Desire.

"Don't worry about calling for a ride. I'll, uh... I'll drive you back to the hotel."

"Okay," I agreed, draining the last of my drink and tossing some bills on the counter for tip, even though I'd already paid and closed the tab.

CHAPTER TWENTY-FOUR

Cade

I DIDN'T KNOW what had possessed me. It was like I was truly someone else. Like some alien had invaded my body like Invasion of the Body Snatchers. And I knew the alcohol wasn't to blame, because I'd literally had only one beer.

No, the intoxication came from Weston Rhodes, who was sitting in my car, staring out my window at the blur of Jasper Springs while I was having an existential crisis.

I wasn't the guy who came on to other guys. I was the guy who liked to be chased. I was *not* the guy who did the catching, whatsoever.

But somehow I'd managed to lure Weston into my web, and I didn't want to let him go.

Ever.

His sophisticated cologne filled the tiny space of the car, and the way his sleeves were rolled up to expose his toned arms made my stomach flip again.

But I was starting to see past Weston's gem-like surface. I was starting to see the mineral compounds that made the beautiful man I didn't want to stop looking at.

I wanted to dive further in, unveil all of his secrets and thoughts. I wanted to know everything there was to know about Weston Rhodes.

Because as I ventured into his dark, murky waters, I realized he wasn't who I thought he was.

He was more than some rich asshole looking to add a notch on his bedpost in town whatever on his list of voyages.

When we'd pulled up to the Palisades, I didn't turn the car off.

Weston turned to me, his green eyes imploring me. "Stay," he said.

One word that held so much meaning it was as heavy as a steel beam.

His eyes pleaded with me, full of wishful desire and dreams. Of promises that others had undoubtedly broken.

I wanted to stay. I wanted to stay forever.

"I want to, but—" I admitted, feeling my throat tighten with anxiety.

But the fundraiser is tomorrow, and I should probably get some rest.

But I don't have a change of clothes.

But I don't want to be a dick.

But I want to stay.

"But what?" Weston asked, turning in his seat.

"I don't even have a change of clothes or—"

"Is that all? Cade, I can get you anything you need or want. You just say the word," Weston said, cocking his head to the side. He seemed utterly confused.

I sighed, turning off the car. I didn't want to waste gas after all, and I could tell this conversation was far from over.

"I don't need you to buy me a new wardrobe, Weston. I don't need all of this," I said as I pointed to the grandiose hotel that looked like something out of a historical drama.

The Palisades was Jasper Springs's

most exquisite building. Everyone and their brother had rented the place for their wedding, or had their baby showers there, and once or twice they even filmed a movie there.

Weston nodded, pursing his lips.

"I'm sorry, Cade, I didn't mean... I just... I don't know how to do *this*."

It was my turn to act shocked and confused.

"Do what Wes?" I breathed, my voice soft in the shared space.

Weston pointed between us. "This. Not control the situation. Not shower you with every expensive toy or piece of clothing you want. Give you whatever it takes to keep you, even if it's just for a night."

He turned to look out the window, and I watched his shoulders fall, watched as he hunched himself up and refused to look at me.

My heart broke to see him like this.

Candid, honest.

So desperate for a love that he'd clearly never had.

"Hey," I said as I reached out and set my hand on his thigh.

He turned slowly, his gaze flicking to where I touched him before he looked back at me.

"I don't need all the fancy bullshit. I just need you," I said honestly, my heart thumping so loudly in my chest I thought he could surely hear it.

He smirked before answering. "And a change of clothes. Obviously."

The words forced themselves out of my mouth without warning. I was running on pure adrenaline, as I'd never felt this emboldened before.

Then again, I'd never had an actual millionaire at my feet begging me to stay the night before either, so I guess that will do wonders for anyone's self esteem.

"Give me like, a half hour, forty minutes. I'll head back to my place, grab some clothes, maybe some ice cream? We can hang out all night, eating ice cream and watching some movies to forget all the bullshit, yeah?" I asked. Hoping he would say yes.

I wasn't entirely sure how to give Weston what he needed, but damned if I didn't want to try. And the only way I knew how to shove off the stress and strain of life was to curl up on my couch and do just as I was proposing. Except, I usually did it alone.

Some things are better with another person.

Weston seemed to relax at my words, nodding.

"Okay," he said, clearly nervous.

"I'll come back, I promise," I said.

He opened the door. "Text me when you're back here?" he asked, standing in the open air, the moonlight shining down on him.

I nodded in response. "Of course," I said as my nerves started to make their way to my heart.

Weston closed the door, and I watched him walk away.

Panic tried to settle in, but I pushed it aside.

I can do this.

It's not like I've never spent the night with anyone, and it doesn't mean we have to have sex.

Did I want that, though?

The fact I couldn't answer no made my entire body flush with heat, and I turned the car on, speeding off in the direction of my house.

CHAPTER TWENTY-FIVE

Cade

I HURRIEDLY PACKED an overnight bag, probably with more shit than I actually needed, and as I stared at the box of condoms in my bedside table, I felt at a crossroads.

If I brought them, it didn't mean I'd have to use them. Plus, Weston had assured me he was diligent about his health and he was clean. I didn't have any reason to believe him, but that little voice inside me did.

I trusted Weston.

I barely knew him, but I was starting to. And he hadn't lied to me yet. In fact it was quite the opposite. He'd been upfront with me since that night at M's Place.

I grabbed the box, just in case.

Better to be prepared than not, right?

I looked at the quiet, dark space of my house, for the first time really feeling the absence of another person.

It had never bothered me as much before. Men came and went in my life, and my house was constant. It would always be here, even when they weren't.

But as I looked around at the crisp, clean, and cozy living room, I wondered what it would be like... to share this place with someone.

But not just any someone...

Weston.

Would he fit in here?

Amongst the Star Wars figurines and the handmade gifts from pet parents?

Would he look just as perfect on my little grey couch with a cup of coffee as he did in Bernard's?

Would he feel at home somewhere like here?

With me?

The thoughts that assaulted me were alarming.

This was a bad idea, wasn't it?

A week ago I would have said yes. But I couldn't quite say that now, not as every inch of me felt pulled toward the Palisades, toward Weston.

So I slung the bag over my shoulder, locked the door, and headed back to my car, thinking the whole way to the hotel that this is it.

This is the moment I lose my goddamn marbles and jump off the cliff.

I could only hope that Weston would be there to catch me, and that I wasn't making a complete mistake.

CHAPTER TWENTY-SIX

Cade

WHEN I SHOWED up to Weston's hotel room, I felt on the edge of a damn precipice. I held two pints of Rocky Road in my hand, wondering if Weston even liked ice cream, or Rocky Road for that matter, pausing before I knocked. But almost as if he could sense me, he opened the door, smiling haughtily.

"You came back."

"I told you I would," I said as I cleared my throat, showing off the ice cream.

"I hope you like Rocky Road," I said as Weston waved me in.

"I like all flavors of ice cream," he said,

flashing me a smirk as he closed the door.

Holy shit, I'm actually doing this.

I dropped my bag on the floor, setting the ice cream down on the bureau.

Weston motioned to a door that connected his room to another.

"You can take the other bed tonight if you like. I don't want you to feel like certain things are... expected," he said the words carefully, clearly. Like he had that first morning when he'd told me sex didn't matter.

And suddenly I understood, that it *did* matter to him.

He just didn't know how to accurately express that, because in his mind it made him unattractive. It made him needy, clingy, and everything that would drive a person away.

Oh, Weston.

I popped open the first container and opened the plastic spoon from its wrapping on the side, handing it to Weston.

"I appreciate that. But maybe for now, we just... relax. Okay?" I asked.

Weston pulled the ice cream from me, our fingers brushing; his warm against my cold hand.

"Okay." He nodded as he dug in.

I watched him slowly pull the spoon out of his mouth, his eyes fluttering in pleasure and he groaned. Immediately, my brain pushed forth the image of him doing such a thing with my cock in place of that spoon.

Fuck, now I'm hard.

That didn't take long.

I grunted in response as I turned away, both to shift my erection and grab my ice cream. Weston plopped himself on the bed, kicking his legs out. I realized at that moment that he'd also kicked his shoes off, and his bright, "Fuck Around & Find Out" socks pulled my attention. It was a quirky thing to see, amidst his finely tailored, dark slacks and his button up shirt.

It was actually kind of cute.

"Nice socks," I teased him.

Weston only wiggled his toes and raised his eyebrows. "That's my motto in life, Cade. Fuck around and find out."

I shook my head as I took my seat next to him.

"You're something else, you know that," I said as Weston turned the tv on, channel flipping. I dove in for a bit of ice cream.

"One hundred percent. And now you know it too," he said with a smile, settling on...

Of course he'd pick Star Wars Phantom Menace.

Could this man be any more perfect?

The movie had already started, so it was in the middle, but I didn't care. I took another bite of my ice cream as Weston did the same.

I leaned in closer, just a bit as the cold set in. Weston stiffened from the contact, as if he was afraid, but of what I wasn't sure.

Instinctively, I curled a little closer, seeking his warmth, and almost immediately he eased up. He wrapped his arm around my shoulders and I yawned.

The Phantom Menace was always boring to me, and I found it hard to stay awake. The low hum of Weston's breath, the rise and fall of his chest, the droning on of the movie dialogue, and a full stomach was too much to fight.

"Go to sleep Cade," Weston whispered.

And I couldn't fight his words, his command. I was really fucking tired.

"Yes, sir," I whispered as I drifted off to

sleep, warm and sated.

The last thought I had before sleep overcame me was that I was falling in love with this man, and that scared me more than any public speaking event.

Because Weston had made it abundantly clear Jasper Springs wasn't his home, but as I drifted off to sleep in his arms, I dared to dream that maybe one day it could be.

CHAPTER TWENTY-SEVEN

Weston

WHEN I WOKE up, I was aware of two things. My arm had gone numb, and Cade was wrapped around me like a damn lemur on the bed. I shifted us, careful not to jostle him too much and wake him.

His lips parted just enough that I could hear tiny soft snores, his dark eyelashes standing out against his sunlit skin. The light of morning bathed him like an angel, and I couldn't help but think that's exactly what he looked like in my arms.

I steadied my breath as I ran my fingers through his soft hair, my heart lifting as he sleepily moaned out a sound of contentment from my touch.

I want to keep you and this moment forever.

However, that was the moment my pain in the ass parents decided to call me. Or more accurately, my pain in the ass father.

The annoying call broke the spell of perfection, and Cade shifted in my arms as I regrettably pulled away.

"Yes, father?" I said probably much harsher than I'd meant to, but I was still a bit tired, and as far as I was concerned it was still too early to deal with Rhodes Family Drama.

I had just woken up, for fuck's sake.

Like the businessman he was, he didn't even address our tense *discussion* at last night's barely eaten dinner. Instead, he just steamrolled right over it, launching into his serious dad tone.

"I'm holding a meeting today on the fifth floor, conference room A. Your presence is mandatory." His tone conveyed all business, commanding and with little room for refusal.

A part of me instinctively wanted to refuse on principle, because there was nothing I hated more than being forced into anything.

Especially by my father.

Fencing lessons, boarding school, a job I didn't think I was qualified for.

But I also knew that my father rarely spoke to me like *this*.

I could count on my hand the number of times he'd sounded so serious, his tone making his order seem absolutely imperative.

Which made me sit up straighter, my muscles tightened. Everything about his words caused panic to form in the pit of my stomach.

This can't be good.

Cade groggily mumbled something beside me, but it was white noise as I tried to focus on finding my own voice.

"I understand," I said, my own voice not betraying how truly worried I was.

If my presence was *mandatory*, I knew this was probably it. The day I'd been dreading since that summer before I'd graduated.

"Be there at ten o'clock. Don't be late," he said curtly, before hanging up on me, leaving me to stew in my panic alone.

The sound of a toilet flushing in the background pulled me from my waking nightmare, reminding me I *wasn't* alone. I turned to see Cade strolling through the doorway, stopping as our eyes met.

I noted the time on the nightstand clock read eight thirty. I had exactly an hour and a half until the damn world came crashing down.

My only thought was I wished I could have spent it with Cade. Curled up under the covers, kissing him until he begged me to stop. Ordering room service and just laying in bed watching terrible hotel movies.

But life just wasn't fucking fair, sometimes.

"Who was that?" Cade asked as I climbed off the bed, pulling off my shirt. I folded it neatly and set it on the left side of my suitcase, doing the same with my slacks until I was down to my briefs. I could feel Cade's eyes on me, the heat of his gaze. I reached for a pair of clean slacks and a lilac silk shirt.

"My father. Unfortunately, I have an early meeting today," I said without inflection.

"Oh, okay," Cade said softly, his voice full of unspoken words.

I wished I could stay and coax out his

truths, but unfortunately I needed to get my shit together and get out the door as soon as possible if I wanted to make it to the Rhodes building on time, and have time to at least grab a coffee or something. The traffic here in the morning was thicker than I'd thought it would be for such a small town.

I pulled on my slacks, buckling my belt with haste. I shimmied into my shirt, buttoning the buttons in the quickest sprint, before taking a seat on the bed to put my socks and shoes on, adjusting my watch.

"I'm really sorry about this, Cade, really. I am. I just—"

"I get it, Weston. Duty calls. I have a job too," he said, but I did not miss the sadness in his voice. I grabbed my deodorant off the nightstand, sprayed myself with my signature cologne, and ran a hand through my messy hair if only to help smooth the "I'd just woken up" look over. I was ready for Rhodes Family Drama in a matter of minutes.

At least on the outside.

Cade turned to me as I headed past him for the door. I stopped, my hand on the doorknob before turning to look back at him and his puppy dog blue eyes.

He looked like someone had eaten the last cookie from the cookie jar, and I hated it.

I hated that such a look was my fault.

Damn it, dad, why couldn't you do this on any other fucking day?

I pulled away from the door for a moment, taking a step toward Cade. He didn't make any sudden movements, instead just watched me intently as I invaded his space until we were close enough I could touch him.

And because I'd always been a damn glutton for punishment, I reached out and set my hand on his hip, pulling him into my space.

He fell into me with ease, without hesitation, as his pristine irises stared into my own.

"I'll see you at the fundraiser today," I said, the words hopeful and a promise all their own.

Cade sighed, his gaze dipping to my lips as he set his hand on my hip, fingernails pushing against the soft silk of my shirt, gripping me with newfound possession.

I liked the feeling, but I didn't have

time to fall into Cade's sexy touch like I wanted to.

That would have to wait for later.

Later is what I should focus on, instead of the immense guilt of abandoning this perfect man right now or this meeting.

"Yeah, yeah, of course," he said calmly, nodding.

I set my hands on the side of his face, my thumb brushing over the soft, pliable flesh of his bottom lip. Between the look of longing in his eyes, the guilt, and the overwhelming *need* to bury myself into Cade until I disappeared, I was powerless to resist him when he leaned up and kissed me.

He ran his hands up my side, heated palms burning little trails of fire along my skin through the silk fabric. I softened from his touch, my shoulders relaxing as I let him coax my tongue into his mouth, as he sucked at my lower lip with a feral heat that I wanted to taste over and over again.

I broke away, breathless.

No one had ever kissed me like *that,* man or woman.

Like I was a damn bloody diamond in the rough.

Like I was *everything.*

"Okay," I said as I pulled away, immediately hating how empty and cold I felt away from his arms, from his magnetic pull.

I opened the door without looking back, because I knew if I did, I would never leave.

CHAPTER TWENTY-EIGHT

Weston

CONFERENCE ROOM A was the biggest conference room in the whole building. While most investors and clients scheduled their meetings for one or two people, and on occasion, with a team, I'd only ever had the chance to see a meeting in Conference Room A once, and that was the summer I'd volunteered.

Then, it had a been a meeting with another firm in the city, Sandusky Security, one of our biggest competitors at the time. My father proposed a truce, a merger of sorts. Thankfully, the other company agreed, but that didn't mean it was an easy one or two person affair. Since we basically bought out the company, that day the entirety of their company, their staff, and the owners had been housed in the room that held a hundred people. Our staff, our executives and those privy to the business side of the merger were all required to be there, for negotiations and for the confirmation of announcement that Sandusky Security and Rhodes Enterprises had become one.

But that didn't compare to the amount of people in the board room today... including my mother, who looked like she was nursing a hangover, with her bug-eyed black sunglasses in a natural lighting room at ten in the morning.

I took my seat next to her begrudgingly, sliding her a bottle of Fiji from the stocked bar in the corner of the conference room.

Dad always liked to have the bar stocked for the big meetings. People were more likely to be agreeable to whatever bullshit you're throwing at them when they were drinking at ten in the morning. And even if they weren't, everyone likes a free drink.

"Thanks, sweetie," she said with a sigh

as she unscrewed the cap, her perfectly manicured nails glinting in the natural light filtering in.

Maybe it was my dread, maybe it was because I'd had a good night's sleep for the first time in a long time, and maybe it was because I was just feeling candid, but whatever the reason was, I eased up next to her as the rest of the suits dwindled in one by one.

"Mom, about last night..."

"It's okay, Weston, we don't have to talk about it," she said with a defeated sigh.

I batted my Fiji water back and forth in my hands, chewing my lip. Despite the anxiety swelling in my stomach, I had the overwhelming inkling to confess the truth to her.

"I... I met someone. Recently," I spoke softly.

She turned to me, peering at me over her shades to show me bright eyes full of shock.

"Weston, honey, don't take this the wrong way, but you meet a lot of people. You're going to have to give me a little more."

I bristled in my seat, knowing this was

a dangerous game to play with her. My mother, as sweet as she could be, could still be quite a gossip hound, and the last thing I wanted was for Cade to end up water cooler chit chat.

But still, I felt the burdening need to be truthful. To lay it out on the table.

My father liked to think I was some playboy asshole, dicking down men that were after our fortune and nothing else, and that was embarrassing for him and the company. And being as I'd never done a thing to correct him, nor had I ever brought anyone into our Rhodes Family Soap Opera, I supposed maybe on some level he was right and I agreed with him. He and my mother didn't know I *wanted* things to change. I wanted someone different, but money complicates things. It always has and it always will.

"I met a *guy*, mom," I said as Cynthia passed out waters to a few of the men pouring in. I noted the time on the clock said it was 9:55 am, and we had a few minutes to spare. My father wasn't there yet, but I knew he liked to be exact with things. He'd waltz in the place at ten and launch into whatever it was he had to say immediately, giving no room for buffering.

My words must have registered for her as her mouth formed a tiny 'o' and she nodded, just as my father came in and shut the door.

His scoured the room, landing on my mother and I with a soft, melancholy look.

I nearly jumped out of my seat when my mother slid her hand over mine.

CHAPTER TWENTY-NINE

Weston

THE ANNOUNCEMENT OF my father's retirement shouldn't have been surprising, but I guess that maybe on some level I hadn't though he'd actually do it. My entire life, my dad's main focus was his company. He'd talked about retiring years ago, but it had fallen to the wayside. He just couldn't give up control, and he didn't *want* to leave his company in the hands of just anyone.

He wanted to leave it with me, and I was not in any way, shape, or form ready to take over a company. Nor did I want to.

I just wanted to live my life. Work my

dumb little job, fuck the pretty assholes who didn't care about me, and experience everything the world had to offer me outside of Jasper Springs.

But as my dad elaborated to the room full of men that it was simply time for him to hand over the reins, I couldn't help but feel nauseous.

He'd said he would do his best to hire the *right* person for the job, the *best* person, whoever that may be. But I think all of us in that room knew it was push come to shove.

Could I really refuse?

Could I say no now that it was really happening?

And then he looked at me. For a brief moment before he wrapped up his speech, he looked at me with a gleam in his eyes.

This wasn't just a planned retirement, no. My father was calling checkmate. He was well and truly putting the ball in my court.

I knew he would entertain the idea of hiring someone else, because my father was many things; organized and ten steps ahead were two of them. But the minute I came to him and said yes, none of those candidates would matter.

Suddenly, I felt like I couldn't breathe. The room was closing in around me and I needed to get out.

I needed to be as far away from Rhodes Enterprises as I could get.

Just as my father opened the floor for questions, I took my leave.

I calmly stood, I'm sure distracting some much better equipped employees than I, and I walked as fast as I could down the hall.

When I heard footsteps behind me, I didn't turn around. Instead, I kept my eye on the elevators, picking up my pace.

"Weston, stop!" my father hollered.

I didn't stop. Instead, I hurried toward the hall, hearing him picking up his own pace.

"I'm not doing this, right now, dad," I said with a huff.

"Then when the hell will you do it?" he growled. I stopped in front of the elevator, hitting the button with rapid aggression.

"There are a hundred people in that room who are far more qualified for this job than me, and you know that," I said boldly.

"On paper, yes. But the heart of this company isn't quarterly reports and product development, and I think somewhere deep down, you know that," he said.

I turned to look at him, that hopeful, wistful look in his eyes filling up with... tears?

My dad *never* cried.

And something about that made my heart break.

I was the worst son on the planet. I didn't deserve any of this. The company, or his unwavering faith that I could do this if he just... *forced* my hand enough.

"I've got a fundraiser to attend," I said as the elevator door opened, and I walked away.

CHAPTER THIRTY

Cade

I LAZILY STROKED the soft fur of an orange and white striped kitten in my lap. Diane called our friends from the Deer Park Rescue, albeit very last minute, but they'd agreed to let us take some kittens to the event to help promote their adoptions.

The tiny kitten pawed at my shirt, stretching her little claws to make biscuits in the folds of the fabric, and I sighed.

I'd been at the event for a couple hours, and although I had several people stop to play with the kittens and ask about the adoptions, as well as take some flyers, stickers, and pens from the hospital, I couldn't help but feel worried for the one person I didn't see.

I knew it was probably selfish of me to expect Weston to show up like the breath of fresh air he was, especially given he'd practically run out the door this morning to make a mandatory meeting at his family's company. But something about his departure, no matter how sound the reason was, left me feeling empty.

He'd said he'd be there, and I wanted to believe him.

But there was also a part of me that knew this was par for the course for me. I'd had a history of falling for assholes who I couldn't really count on.

I gazed down at the kitten who had stopped making biscuits, and was now curled up in the folds of my shirt, snoozing away.

I guessed she was bored of waiting too.

"Why so gloomy, sunshine?" a familiar voice pulled me from my thoughts.

I looked up to see Mitch, complete with camera, as usual. I swear he never left home without the damn thing.

"I'm not gloomy..." I said, even though I knew the words were a lie.

Mitchell kneeled to take some photos of the kittens in their pen.

"You are a shit liar, Cade. Seriously."

I rolled my eyes, but decided it was better to just be honest than make something up.

It wasn't like Weston was around anyway to hear me.

"Weston said he'd be here today. At the fundraiser."

Mitchell looked up from his spot on the ground.

"You haven't seen him?" Mitchell asked, reaching in the pen to stroke a grey and white striped kitten on its head with his finger.

"No..."

"He's been schmoozing around all afternoon. I think I saw him over by the park like ten minutes ago."

My blood chilled, and I was worried maybe my anxieties were right. Maybe he was ignoring me.

Had I been wrong about him?

It wouldn't have been the first time I'd looked at a man with rose tinted glasses, but...

Last night, as we cuddled on the bed together, drowning our stress in ice cream and Star Wars, I thought that maybe he *was* different. Maybe, just maybe this time I'd gotten it right.

"Earth to Cade," Mitchell said, and I realized I'd completely spaced out.

"Sorry, Mitch, I—"

"You want me to man the desk a bit? You can walk around and grab something to eat, maybe find your new boy toy," he teased.

I couldn't help the flush of blood into my cheeks at his insinuation.

"It's not like that. It's—"

"Then what is it like, Cade? Hmmm? I've known you a long time, and I've never seen you get all doe-eyed like this over anyone. Even the assholes that came before. For God's sake, when Dawson broke up with you, you didn't even bat an eye. But this guy has you all up in arms because you just haven't *seen* him? If I didn't know any better, I'd say you were in love."

His words hit me like a freight train.

I'd only known Weston for barely three days. Surely it was impossible to fall in love with someone you hardly knew for seventy-two hours. This was real life, not a Disney movie.

But as Mitch's words settled on me, infiltrating my walls, I knew they held truth.

I was head over heels in love with Weston Rhodes, and that was terrifying.

Because giving anyone that kind of power over your heart, especially when you weren't sure where you stood... was scary.

"Okay, maybe you don't need to leave..." Mitchell said as he stood.

"One loverboy coming straight at you, twelve o clock," Mitchell cooed as he snapped a picture of Weston amongst the crowd.

My heart lifted at the sight. Seeing his lilac sleeves rolled up, two buttons popped, his dark hair blowing in the wind. He was breathtaking set against the varied trees and flowers, looking every bit the man of my dreams.

Was I the man of his?

I didn't know.

I didn't know what I was to Weston. After all, he'd been clear he was only here on business, and eventually that business would end.

We'd been lucky the event in Jasper Springs had been so successful.

Successful enough that Rhodes had decided to put on two additional events, the one today and one at the end of the week in Paradise. But the events couldn't go on forever. Eventually, Weston would have to leave, and I wasn't sure where that left us.

Would I be just a Jasper Springs fling?

Some memory he looked back fondly on?

A transition from one stage to the next?

From one bed to the next?

"Hey," he said as he approached my booth, sliding his hands in his pockets.

I stood, holding the sleepy kitten tight to my chest, letting my fingers slide over the soft fur to keep myself steady.

I looked up at his dark, green eyes, and the world around me blurred.

Yeah, I was definitely in love with Weston.

There was no question.

Fuck me.

"Hey," I said, feeling my throat go dry.

"I'm sorry I didn't come find you earlier, but things have just been... Well, it was a rough morning."

"Oh," I said, suddenly at a loss for

words. My brain screamed a thousand things at me.

Tell him the truth, tell him how you feel.

Ask him how he feels.

Kiss him.

Weston's gaze fell to the kitten in my arms.

"Make a new friend?" he said, flashing me a grin.

I didn't miss how it lit up his eyes. I stroked the soft, warm kitten as I swallowed nervously.

"Let me make this morning up to you?" he asked, his gaze finally leaving my fingers and meeting mine.

There were a hundred things I wanted to say, but instead all that came out of my mouth was, "You do an awful lot of making up."

Weston's shoulders fell and instantly I felt like an asshole. I hadn't meant it to sound as harsh as it did, but I guess I was still a little melancholy from this morning. Everything had been so perfect, and then just like before, we'd both been thrust back into the world of responsibility.

Before I could speak, apologize for sounding like an absolute ass, Weston ran a hand through his hair, his eyebrows furrowing.

"I'd like to change that, you know," he said gently.

The kitten stirred in my arms, yawning and stretching.

"A fresh start?" I asked, feeling all the negativity suddenly draining from me.

Weston reached out to rub the kitten between its ears, and she purred like a damn motor from his touch.

Same kitten, same.

"You can pick the place," Weston said smoothly.

I watched his fingers gently stroke her fur, watched the sadness fall on his face, and all the disappointment, all the worry and concern faded away like it hadn't been there at all.

I'd been so busy thinking about myself and my own self-sabotaging feelings that I hadn't once thought about how Weston must have felt.

Maybe he didn't want to leave either.

Maybe he needed this, needed *me* just as bad as I needed him.

So I decided in that moment, that even if this ended in flames, that for the time being I would be everything he needed.

For however long it lasted.

Because against all odds, I loved this man.

"Fine. Grab your phone," I instructed.

Weston's lips tweaked up in the corner.

"I like you bossy, you know," he said, his voice husky as he stopped petting the little motor in my arms, sliding out his phone. He cast me a dark, sexy look that made my stomach flip.

I spouted off my address, keeping my face devoid of emotion. As far as he knew, it was just another restaurant in town, a café, or something like Bernard's. After all, Weston didn't spend much time here, so there was no way for him to know the address I'd given him was actually my house.

"Meet me there at say... seven o clock?" I asked, sternly but also just in case he actually *did* have some sort of plans or business dinner.

He smiled sexily in return.

"It's a date," he said, just as a group of teenage girls caught sight of the kittens, running over with loud, shrieking squeals.

"It's a date," I said as he walked away,

smiling from ear to ear.
    And it's going to be the best date ever.

CHAPTER THIRTY-ONE

Weston

I THOUGHT THERE had to be some mistake. Though Cade had been secretive about where he'd picked, a part of me thought I must have genuinely misheard him. Because when my Uber showed up to a quaint, little brick house complete with a white picket fence and lawn gnomes in the front yard, I was sure I had to have missed something.

Instinctively, I pulled out my phone to double check the message, as I texted Cade to tell him I was about five minutes away. But just as I queued up my messenger to tell him I'd be a few minutes late because my driver had obviously taken a wrong turn, I saw him.

Standing on the porch in a blue polo, hands in his dark wash jeans, with a smirk.

The little brat.

He'd actually gotten one over on me, and I let out a small chuckle in the space of the car. I slid my phone back in my pocket before leaving the car, taking my time to walk up the sidewalk until I'd reached his porch.

"Are you taking me somewhere special?" I teased him.

Cade cocked his head to the side as he set his hand on my hip, tugging me closer.

"Of course. You deserve only the best, right?" Cade teased me back.

I slid my arm around his waist, pulling him closer to me. His bright blue eyes sparkled with mischief and I was powerless to resist crushing my lips against his with appreciation. He tasted like strawberries and champagne, and it was divine.

"Starting the party without me?" I purred against his soft lips.

Cade gazed up at me with intrigue.

"I can't help that every time I know I'm

going to see you, I get a little nervous."

My heart lifted at his words.

They were honest, endearing, and carried a hint of vulnerability I'd never known anyone to exhibit to me romantically before.

"I make you nervous?" I asked as I brought my lips to his again.

Cade groaned into my mouth, and I could feel him hardening against me, the sensation of his arousal against my own sudden erection making me see stars.

Instinctively, I let my lips wander to his jaw, nibbling, sucking at the flesh until he was practically putty in my arms.

"Fuck yes," he breathed as he relaxed in my hold.

I pulled away suddenly, taking stock of the look on his face. His swollen lips, flushed cheeks. My blood raced beneath my skin, my stomach tying into knots as I took in the beauty and the aura of the man in front of me.

"The feeling's mutual," I said, awestruck.

Cade shook his head, dispelling the momentary lapse of sanity, sliding his hand in mine as he pulled me toward the open door.

"Come in," he said, his voice catching a little to convey he really *was* nervous.

A part of me found that endearing. That I could have such an effect on anyone, let alone someone as perfect as Cade.

Inside the house, I was immediately struck with the scent of garlic, butter, and perfectly aged parmesan reggiano. My mouth watered almost instantly.

Not to mention the cozy atmosphere. While there was a fireplace, it looked like it was walled off. Instead of logs, long stemmed metal candlesticks were strewn across the bottom, and I had to appreciate the ornate mahogany mantle that looked like something out of the forties.

The living room itself wasn't huge, but it was full of character. Little Star Wars figurines, bright, woven blankets, and candles strewn about nearly everywhere, but none lit.

The couch alone begged me to jump in and take a long needed nap. Combined with the scent of butter and cheese, I felt like I'd died and gone to heaven. I stood there like an idiot, while Cade left me to my devices, coming back with a glass of fizzy pink champagne, complete with sliced strawberry at the bottom of the flute.

"Are we celebrating something?" I asked.

Cade smirked. "The opening of Cade's Cafe, of course."

"The place seems quite promising."

"And you haven't even had the best part yet," he said as he flung a kitchen towel over his shoulder as he headed into the kitchen, and I followed him without question.

His kitchen was barely a quarter the size of the one in the Rhodes Family home, but somehow it felt more open and warm than any other I'd been in. I took a seat at the island, clutching my drink as I watched him toss food in the pan, manning a couple different pots and pans with ease. The island itself was set for two, complete with little bowls of salad in bamboo bowls that had black painted paw prints on them.

Perhaps there was a time I would have found such a thing kitchsy, or tacky even, but here in Cade's home, it was cute. Endearing, even.

I watched him in awe, as he moved

about his kitchen, watched the muscles in his arm flex as he flipped things in pans, taking sight of his firm ass and the way the dark wash jeans hugged his form.

Was there anything this man couldn't do?

"I hope you like risotto, because if not, you're screwed," he said with a light laugh.

I set my drink down as I swiveled back and forth on the barstool.

"I have many acquired tastes, I can assure you," I said as I watched him spoon the mixture into a deep, white bowl. "You didn't have to do this, you know."

He walked over with a bowl of fresh risotto. It smelled *divine,* and when he sprinkled fresh herbs on top from a small dish on the island, I realized without a doubt that this man was absolutely perfect, and as he sat down across from me with his own plate, smiling genuinely at me as he picked up his fork, he said, "I know, but I wanted to."

And at that moment, I knew.

Cade was as good as they came. He was passionate, smart, attractive, and had a heart that was full of so much love it would have been hard for me to *not* fall in love with him.

Because as I watched Cade blow across the steaming hot food on his fork, I knew without a doubt, I was falling in love with this man.

This man who seemed to make the rest of the world fall away, who seemed to be able to draw out the darkest parts of me and make everything... okay.

"My dad, uh, announced his retirement today," I said as I took a stab at my food.

"Is that a good thing?" He took a sip of his champagne.

The glow of the kitchen light lit up his soft blonde hair like a halo.

"He wants me to take over the company," I said the words out loud for the first time since this morning, feeling their weight. I expected them to be heavy, like steel beams, but in the presence of Cade, they didn't feel quite as heavy.

"And that's not something you want?" he pressed, taking another bite of food.

I took a bite myself, relishing in the smooth, buttery texture, and the taste was absolutely perfect.

"Oh my God, Cade, this is *amazing*." I

groaned my pleasure as I hurriedly went for another forkful.

"Thanks. I know it's not like authentic or five star, but... sometimes a homemade meal is nice too, you know."

I didn't know. Not really. When I thought about all the homemade food I'd had, it wasn't really quite like this.

Margo made most of our food, and my parents were always obsessed with healthy foods and gourmet stuff that didn't really appeal to me. I would have been fine with a pepperoni pizza, but as it was I didn't even have cheesy, junky pizza until I'd moved into the city on my own.

No one had ever made me dinner before... romantically. I'd never gone on a date that didn't end in a large bill, up until I'd come here to Jasper Springs.

"I just don't know if I'm right for the job," I said as I took another bite of my dinner.

"And no one has ever made me dinner before, so you're definitely getting a five star Michelin review from me," I said as I finished my bowl in two more, appreciative bites.

Cade looked at me in shock.

"You're kidding, right?" he asked.

I shook my head. "Wish I was, but no. Most of my exes preferred to dine out at the swankiest restaurants and bars as opposed to sitting in and ordering room service, and my parents never cooked. We had staff for that."

"I'm sorry, I didn't mean to sound ignorant." Cade set his fork down, reaching his hand across the table to cover mine.

"You didn't. I promise. It's just... you're right, it *is* nice. This whole place is nice, and you..."

"If you say I'm nice, I'm going to have to take your drink away," Cade teased me.

"You're perfect. How in the hell are you still single?

I watched as Cade blushed six shades of red.

"Well, there is this guy..." he said shyly, avoiding my gaze, and immediately my blood ran cold.

Life had always managed to knock me on my ass when I least expected it, so in theory if Cade really was interested in someone else, that would have been my luck, but the way he looked up at me from under his lashes told me there was no one else.

There was only... me.

Oh, Cade...

"Really?" I said, deciding to play his game.

"Tell me about this guy, is he an ass?"

Cade shook his head as he collected our bowls.

"Mmm, I thought maybe he was at first, but he's kind of surprised me, actually," he said.

"Oh really? How so?" I asked as I followed him to the sink.

I watched as he set the bowls in the sink, noting he couldn't see me, or my hands that settled on the edge of his counter alongside him.

He turned around, realizing he was trapped between his counter and my body. His eyes lit up with mischief and excitement, a smile ghosting his lips.

"Well, he seems to be kind of a loyal family guy, and he's a pretty good singer, not to mention he's hot as hell and brings out a side of me I didn't know existed."

"Is that so?" I whispered as Cade settled his hands around my waist, pulling me closer, flush against him. His fingers dipped below my waistband at my back, drawing little circles against my skin.

His eyelashes fluttered as he nodded.

"And I think..." He swallowed, his gaze dipping to my lips. His breathing caught in his throat, and he seemed nervous.

"What? What do you think?" I asked, imploring his gaze with my own.

Cade looked up at me with clear, blue eyes and in them I could see a hundred unsaid words, a thousand unspoken emotions.

I'd always dreamed of someone who would look at me the way he did that night in his kitchen.

I was head over heels in love with Cade Green.

Because when I looked in his eyes, I knew that the sky was the limit.

"I think I might be falling for him," he whispered, his words shaky.

I reached out, pushing some stray strands of golden hair behind the shell of his warm ear.

"Are you scared of falling, Cade?" I whispered, even though we didn't need to. However, it felt as though the words themselves were the size of great beasts.

"I'm just scared he doesn't feel the same." Cade leaned his cheek into my palm.

"I think he does," I said as I leaned my forehead against his, taking a deep breath.

I'd never considered myself a courageous man on any account, but I'd also never been afraid of wearing my heart on my sleeve. I'd given so much of myself, my body, and my money to the wrong people in hopes of one day striking gold, that I'd never considered that love, real love, couldn't be bought.

It was unearthed beneath rubble and dirt, it was born out of fate and circumstances beyond our control.

It was found where one least expected it.

Cade's entire body relaxed as I slid a hand around his waist, pulling him close until I couldn't stand it anymore.

I leaned down and took his lips like they were the dessert I'd been waiting for, for a thousand years.

Cade sank into my hold, wrapping his arms around my neck as he kissed me back, his lips and tongue still carrying a hint of buttery cheese flavor.

And when we broke away, Cade looked at me with a happiness that made my heart want to burst.

I never thought I'd ever be capable of making someone smile like that.

"It wouldn't be a date without a movie to follow," he said sweetly as he gently pushed me back.

I couldn't help but smile in return.

CHAPTER THIRTY-TWO

Weston

ALL THE ASSUMPTIONS I'd had about Cade's couch turned out to be true. It was the softest couch I'd ever had the pleasure of being sucked into.

Cade relaxed with his legs propped up on his ottoman, complete with adorable bunny slippers, one hand behind his head, completely in his element as he focused on the actors on screen.

I couldn't tell you what was happening or even what movie we watched.

Because I couldn't take my eyes off him.

The light of the television bathed him

in an ethereal glow, and I scooted closer to him. The motion pulled his attention away for a moment.

"You okay?" he asked, taken by the sudden movement.

Being this close to him, my arm stretched over his stomach, my head on his shoulder was too much.

I nodded as I took in the sight of him, looking down at me.

When we were upright, I had a good few inches on him, being nearly six foot one myself, but in bed, or on a couch, I could cuddle up close to Cade and look up at *him*.

Like the damn angel he was.

I nodded in response. I was better than okay. I felt amazing.

I pulled him down to my lips, taking him by surprise. I loved kissing Cade, loved how his lips felt plush against my own, how he'd slowly let his tongue breach mine, stroking it until he elicited little groans of pleasure from my mouth, just from his kiss alone.

I wanted to kiss him as much as I could, among other things.

It occurred to me at that moment, as Cade slipped his tongue in my mouth and pulled me closer with his free arm that was wrapped around my shoulders, that while our first meeting had ended with me fucking Cade until he begged me to let him come, we hadn't been physical since. Part of that was on me, because while I wanted to fuck Cade's beautiful mouth and asshole every time I saw him, I was trying to be *good.*

I was trying to be a man deserving of him.

But something in between us had shifted during that time. The tables had somehow turned.

I pulled Cade closer, wrapping my leg over his hip. The movie in the background droned on as Cade instinctually ground his cock against my stomach, as his tongue probed mine with hurried motion, as he bit at my lower lip.

"I'm better than okay," I said breathlessly as I pushed back against him, settling him against his cushions. I straddled his lap, my cock straining against my jeans. I grabbed his face in my hands, kissing him with all that I was.

"You can tell me to stop if you don't want to—" I breathed as I looked down at his face, full of emotion and desire.

He looked slightly torn, but also... *hopeful.*

"I want to," he breathed, his voice shaking again with nerves.

"But?"

"No *but,* Wes. I want you. I've wanted you since that night at M's Place, since the morning I woke up with you next to me, I just... needed some time to process everything. I didn't... I didn't know if you would stay."

Something in his voice called to my soul in a way no one else had ever done.

Did I want to stay?

Here, in Jasper Springs?

With Cade?

Running my father's company?

The fact I couldn't say no entirely made me feel like for the first time in my life, I didn't know what I was capable of.

I only knew that in the arms of Cade Green, I felt like I could do anything. So that's what I focused on.

"And now?" I asked as I gazed down at perfect, crystalline eyes.

"Will you stay?" he asked, licking his lips. "Tonight? Will you stay? With me?" His eyes searched mine for answers I wasn't sure I knew myself, but for the moment I said the one that felt the truest.

"Yes," I said, sliding my hand down his chest, resting my fingers at the hem of his pants. His cock twitched beneath me, poking my thigh from where I straddled him.

"How could I not when your couch is the coziest couch I've ever been on?" I teased him.

Cade smirked as he rested his hand on my ass, pulling me against him with teasing force. His eyes lit up with desire.

"Besides, I don't think I'm quite done making things up to you," I said as my fingers deftly unhooked his belt. His gasp of breath gave me goosebumps. I slowly tugged his jeans and boxers down just enough that his cock could spring free.

"If you make up this much, we may need some couples counseling," he taunted me, but all laughs dissipated in the air when I stared into his beautiful eyes, never breaking his gaze.

And spit in my hand.

I lathered my saliva along my fingers before teasing his entrance as I positioned myself between his knees. His pants shimmied down his legs from the movement.

Instantly, Cade flexed and arched his back from the shock of the sensation as I let my spit-covered fingers tease him, massaging the tight skin.

"Holy fuck, Wes, I—"

"Are you okay? Do you want me to stop?" I asked, half worried I'd misread his desire.

Cade shook his head. "No, absolutely not. Please don't stop," he breathed hurriedly, desire on his tongue more than prevalent.

I continued to stroke the taut skin at his hole with my fingertip, sliding over the puckered hole, teasing his entrance.

Cade thrust himself against me, seeking more of the friction, and I slid my forefinger in a little further.

I stole a glance at his face, which had gone a little slack as he closed his eyes, thrusting his hips, his gleaming dick in the air.

And when I took his swollen head in my mouth, he cried out a string of curses, but I didn't stop until he was in the back of my throat. His asshole clenched my finger like a vice and I started to build my pace. The sleek, wet sound of sucking melded with the slip and slide of my lubricated finger, and just when I felt I'd stretched him enough, I slid another in.

"Oh God, Wes, please, I..."

I hollowed my cheeks, knowing it wouldn't be long. I could feel his cock pulsing, throbbing in my mouth, the saltiness of his precum coating my tongue.

"I'm going to go any second, I—" His voice got all tight, all screwed up right before he came.

Warm, salty cum filled my mouth, and I swallowed it down like the desperate, thirsty son of a bitch I was. I wanted to make Cade feel as good as he made me feel on every level, including the physical.

His cock softened as he caught his breath, and I licked the remaining drops of his sweetness from his head as I came up for air.

Cade looked down at me from where he sat, his eyes full of lust and fire.

"Okay, I think that about sums up my groveling. Think I'm done now," I said with a smirk, wiping some of his mess from the corner of my mouth.

Cade sat up, pulling me against his wet cock, smothering me in a possessive, hot kiss that knocked *me* on my ass.

I opened my mouth without warning, groaning as Cade's tongue probed mine. He moaned in response, and I thought I could see literal stars.

His hands rushed at my belt and he slid his palm down the front of my pants with a welcome aggression, grabbing at my thick, aching cock. The motion pushed my pants to my ankles, leaving me in nothing but my briefs, feeling tight and constrained.

"You don't play fair," he whispered against my lips.

I snickered against his mouth and then moaned into his kiss in response as I thrust my leaking cock against his hand, separated by the thin fabric of my briefs.

"What are you going to do about it, good boy?"

Cade shoved my briefs down to my knees before grabbing me by my hips and upending me onto the couch cushions with a forceful flip. He shook off the rest of his pants as I did the same. My cock bobbed like a beacon in the night, guiding Cade and his mouth to us like the northern star.

"Maybe I'm going to punish you," he growled, but his voice didn't shake at all.

In fact, it was the clearest, sternest tone I'd heard him take yet.

Well, damn. Color me surprised. Our good boy might have a little Dom in him after all.

I leaned back on my elbows, propping myself up so I could look at him while he licked the bead of precum off my tip. His wet, pink tongue licked me from balls to head, slowly, taking in just the tip, teasing me, taunting me. His right hand cupped my balls while his left stroked me slowly.

I thrust my throbbing cock against his lips, painting his mouth with another round of clear, wet arousal.

"Oh yeah? Joke's on you, sweetheart. I like to be the bad guy."

Cade didn't miss a beat as he slipped his right hand beneath my balls, teasing my entrance, much like I had with him, and just as I thought he was going to do the same, he pulled them away, leaving my insides wanting.

Well, that's not fair.

Instead, his heated eyes burned into mine, and he straddled my hips. My gaze dipped to his hand, which was now palming *his* already semi-hard cock.

The sight of him, naked from the waist down, pink, swollen cock in his palm as he looked at me was a beautiful torment.

I'd never wanted *anything* quite this bad. I reached for my own cock, but to my surprise, Cade swatted it away.

"I didn't say you could touch yourself," he said mischievously.

Oh, if this is the game you want to play, sweetheart, I am so in.

I can be your good boy too.

I feigned embarrassment, embellishing on the role if only for Cade and his enjoyment.

I enjoyed watching him like this, and I liked the idea of him being in control.

In all the years I'd been with men, I was always the one on top. The one calling the shots, the one commanding them to submit to me.

But looking at Cade from beneath his steel thighs, I wanted to be good.

I wanted to obey him, because I knew it would bring him so much pleasure.

And if he was happy, well...

Maybe I could find some happiness in that too.

"But I'm so full, I need to come," I embellished, playing right along. I watched his eyes dilate, watched as his cock twitched as I said the words. I had him, hook, line, and sinker.

"Not until I tell you to," he said as he let go of his cock, which was now thick and full, wetness already starting to pebble at the tip.

He was a natural.

He shifted his weight, and his position, until his length bobbed against my dick. Then he looked *me* straight in the eye, and spit into *his* hand, slapping his palms together to baste them in his spit before he wrapped both hands around our cocks.

The warmth of his palm, the wetness of his spit, and the rigidity of his hardness as he thrust his cock slowly against my own was maddening. I lifted my hips, thrusting against his hand, my aching cock needing the friction. Somewhere in the distance I heard my phone ringing, but I ignored it. Whoever it was, it could wait.

"Please," I rasped.

Cade picked up the pace, stroking us both with a hurried rhythm.

"Please, what?" he asked, licking his lips, gazing down at me with those perfect blue eyes full of lust and need, lips still swollen from kissing me.

"Please, Cade, make me come," I begged.

I kind of liked it, if I was being honest.

Being the bottom, my pleasure beholden to the golden god above me.

Though Cade didn't make it, I couldn't very well be disappointed.

Because as he erupted, his warm release spread over the both of us, only adding to the slick, wetness of his saliva.

I thrust my hips madly against him until I too came with a force that had my vision going white. Instinctively, I grabbed onto Cade, wrapping my arms around his neck and pulled him to me for a deep, passionate kiss as he let go. The motion as he leaned down trailed a mixed mess of cum along both of our stomaches, but I didn't care. I wrapped my legs around his hips, thrusting against his softening, wet cock, and I knew nothing would ever be the same again.

CHAPTER THIRTY-THREE

Cade

I AWOKE ON my couch to the sound of a ringtone I certainly didn't recognize.

I blinked, taking in my surroundings. Weston slept soundly beside me on the couch, under one of the many blankets. The phone vibrated and sounded against the table, and I realized it was his phone.

"Weston," I groaned as I reached for the phone, tossing it to him.

He roused, grabbing the phone as he groggily answered me.

"Cade, what..." Then his entire body stiffened as he answered.

"Yes?" His voice had gone from lazy in the morning, to serious and commanding again.

Work calls, obviously.

I swung my legs over the couch, my morning erection aching and full. I needed to take a piss, and then I needed a shower. I watched as Weston slid his briefs back on, brushing off the dried fluids of...

All the memories of last night, of our date, and our Netflix & chill session came rushing back to me. This time I didn't feel guilty or worried, though. This time when the blood rushed into my cheeks I felt... *happy*. Like I wanted to do it all over again.

The dinner, the laughing, the kissing.

The opening up of feelings.

The sex.

That first time we'd fucked, neither of us were properly coherent enough to really be present. Our inhibitions were down, sure. After all I *did* let him fuck me.

But last night was different. Not only were we both *present* for the experiences, but it felt like something deeper than that.

It didn't feel like mindless, sloppy sex with a stranger.

It felt like blinding, fulfilling sex with a

partner.

All my lines were becoming blurred with Weston Rhodes and I wasn't sure I wanted them to be clear anymore.

Not when there was so much beauty and love in the haze.

I made my way to the bathroom, relieving myself before washing off remnants of our dried spend that was all over my stomach. I padded out of the bathroom to my bedroom, grabbing a pair of clean grey sweatpants.

When I came back out, Weston was gone.

I called out, thinking maybe he'd just gone somewhere else to talk, there was no answer. I opened the door, catching the sight of him getting into a car, and before I could speak out, he was off.

Gone without so much as a goodbye.

Had I been wrong about Weston?

Had what we shared been in my head?

My heart broke as the negative thoughts of *'I told you so'* brushed forth and I slammed my fist against the brick, not hard enough to break, but enough that it made my knuckles sore.

At that moment, my phone went off, my alarm blaring at me to get up and get ready for work. I sighed, relenting for the moment as I headed back in the house, to my shower to wash off the pain, the sadness and the reality that I'd fucked up.

Again.

So much for a fresh start.

CHAPTER THIRTY-FOUR

Cade

AT WORK, DIANE sat at the desk, a serious look on her face.

"Everything okay?" I asked as I set my Dunkin Donuts iced coffee down. She looked pale.

"Something go wrong with the fundraiser, or..."

"No, it's, uh... the fundraiser's postponed," she said calmly.

"Oh, okay..."

"The CEO of Rhodes Enterprises had a heart attack last night. He'd announced his retirement, but no replacement has been named yet, so..."

My blood chilled.

How could I have been so selfish, so self-centered?

No wonder Weston had left without a word of goodbye.

No kid wants to get *that* call about their parents, and that's just the ones who don't have parents trying to convince them to run the family business.

Which happens to make millions.

"Oh shit, Diane, I'm sorry, I—" I slide out my phone immediately as she sighs.

"I mean, it's okay, we had two fundraisers, and while I haven't counted the donations yet from last night, I'm sure... I'm sure we'll be fine if they cancel the one on Friday."

I could hear the sadness and the disappointment in her voice. Despite the fact I didn't care for working the booths, I couldn't deny that the events had really good results. High turnouts, and the first event alone had brought in almost five thousand dollars. All that would go toward the hospital, toward care for animals who needed life saving surgeries and care credit funds as well as our rescue friends.

In fact, I'd wager that Rhodes

Enterprises had helped us bring in more money in two events than we'd been capable of doing on our own in the last two years.

I texted Weston immediately, worried for him and what he must be going through.

Are you okay? I texted, immediately sending another, *I heard about your dad.*

Weston texted back, *No. I'm not.*

My heart broke for him. *Tell me what you need.*

I'd said the words because I knew he was hurting, knew he must be worried sick about his dad regardless of their personal issues.

I wasn't expecting his text back to say, *You. I need you.*

I looked up at Diane.

"Diane, I know I just came in but…"

She looked at me with a smirk.

"You think I don't know about you and the Rhodes kid?" she said, shaking her head.

I felt frozen in place. How…

She must have sensed my confusion, because she sighed. "Anyone with eyeballs can see the tension between you two in that photo in the paper. Plus all the ladies in town are talking about it. You have been seen together quite a bit...” Diane twisted her lips.

Busted.

“It just sort of... happened,” I said. It wasn't a lie, but... how else could I explain who or what Weston was to me. Sure, we'd admitted that we had feelings for one another, but it wasn't like we'd declared our undying love or anything, but a part of me wished I had.

“I'm sure your boyfriend is a mess, so I'm going to be nice, just this once, Cade. You've done a lot for me this week, especially with the events. I'm more than equipped with a full staff here today. Take the day off. I know you're already off tomorrow, so just... do what you need to do and I'll see you on Saturday, yeah?” she said kindly.

I grabbed my coffee, twirling my keys in my hand.

“Thank you, Diane,” I said with the utmost appreciation.

“Mhmm. Don't mention it loverboy. Go be the hero of your story today,” she said with a wink and I was out the door in seconds.

When I got to the car, I texted Weston

immediately.

Can you meet me at Penn's Bakery? Grab some coffee?

It was like an eternity until he'd messaged me back, and I started to fear the worst.

Be there in ten minutes.

I sped off in the direction of Penn's Bakery, my heart in my throat.

I had no idea what to do or how I was going to help.

All I knew was that I needed Weston just as bad as he needed me, and if there was something I could do, even if it was meeting up over coffee and telling him everything would be okay, even though I didn't know it would be... that was what I would do.

Because I loved him.

I wanted to be everything he needed me to be and then some.

Because he was so much more to me.

Weston made me come alive. He inspired me, pushed me, and brought out parts of me I wanted to explore with great depth. I wasn't sure what the future held for us, but I knew as I hurried my ass over to Penn's Bakery, that I didn't care where the road led me.

EVIE RILEY

As long as Weston was there too, I knew everything would be all right.

CHAPTER THIRTY-FIVE

Cade

I WALKED INTO Penn's Bakery to see Weston sitting in the corner booth, looking like a lost puppy. I slid into the seat across from him.

"Have you eaten anything?" I asked, noting he looked a little pale.

He shook his head. "No."

"Are you hungry?" I asked, going into crisis management mode, as Dawson would call it.

"I mean, sort of..." he said with a huff.

"Stay here," I commanded as I got up, heading over to the bakery counter.

"Cade..." Weston groaned.

I shot him a look that froze him in place.

"Hush. You need food. Preferably something with a lot of sugar," I said, easing up on the last word. I hadn't meant to sound so tense or bossy, but that was becoming more of a thing the longer I was around Weston. It was like I'd finally found my voice.

"Yes, sir," he said with a light smile. The words warmed my very soul.

I took my time ordering us both some fruit filled croissants and coffee, and in no time we were both diving into the sweet confectionary delights and caffeine like they would heal all wounds.

"Is he going to be okay, your dad?" I asked, setting down my coffee.

Weston turned his dark eyes at me, nodding, his lips pressed in a thin line.

"Yeah. Doc thinks he'll probably make a full recovery, but he needs to stay away from stressful situations."

I nodded in response. "So, I guess that means he's not visiting the old family business any time soon."

Weston nodded. "I'm sure they're all running around like chickens today. He only announced his retirement yesterday, it was hardly any time to get *anything* in order," Weston said as he took a sip of his coffee.

"What will they do? Without a current CEO? Is there someone they'll appoint interim, or..."

Weston shrugged. "I'm not sure, actually. But I should probably stop by at least to see if there's something I can do to make the transition easier. You know, for everyone involved..."

I realized at that moment, maybe before Weston ever did, that despite what he said, he did care.

He didn't think he was fit for the job, because in his eyes he wasn't perfect. He wasn't his father. But maybe he didn't have to be.

Maybe all he had to be was honest, caring, and compassionate.

I reached across the table, taking his hand. He didn't jump or shift. Instead, he squeezed my fingers as he interlaced his with mine.

"We're going to get through this, you know. You're going to get through this," I said, forcing him to meet my gaze. Weston's eyes looked a little glassy, as if he was on the verge of tears.

I would have wiped every one away if he needed me to.

"I don't know if I can do this," he said, breaking my gaze.

Though my own insecurities threatened to rise up at his words, I knew he wasn't talking about us.

Weston was feeling overwhelmed, anxious, and lost. And I knew a thing or two about feeling like that.

"You can. *I* know you can. And you don't have to do it alone," I promised him. He seemed to process my words, nodding slowly as he chewed on them.

"Okay," he said shakily.

I squeezed his hand for good measure. "Okay," I said, letting go.

CHAPTER THIRTY-SIX

Weston

I STOOD IN the front foyer of Rhodes Enterprises, feeling more nervous than I'd ever been before.

Not because I knew the employees inside were probably scrambling and trying to get things smoothed out between all that had happened—the announcement, the fundraiser stuff, the hiring process and postings, the day to day operations of Rhodes.

My father had plenty of people underneath him who he trusted to man the fort while he was gone on vacation or off in another state or something on business, but this was like every employee's nightmare. The boss drops a bombshell, then disappears and there's no instructions or nothing in place to keep things running smoothly.

But still, I just felt like it was the right thing to do.

I'd never seen my dad look so... unlike himself. Pale, a little frail, and like he was exhausted. Not just from his job, but from life.

My mother assured me everything would be fine, to her best ability. Though her puffy, red eyes told me she was just as worried and concerned as I was.

You never know who you are or what you're made of until you're forced to find out. I thought I'd be the person to walk away, to run when my heart and my mind threatened to pull me under the dark, terrifying waves of doubt and worry.

But instead, I found myself channeling Cade apparently, when all I'd said was, "Tell me what you need."

I'd expected them both to tell me, "For you to take over," or something along those lines. With my dad in the hospital, it would have been the perfect time to take advantage of my vulnerability, but... they only said they needed me.

So as I bustled through the hallways of Rhodes, checking on employees and delivering donuts and coffee to each floor, as I ran from conference room to office fetching papers from the printer, and answered calls in my father's office, even if it was only to say, "Thank you for your concerns," I couldn't stop thinking about the fundraiser, which I'd taken upon myself to reinstate. It just didn't sit right with me that the thing would be in limbo or cancelled, when our company was well within its means to continue the event. It had surprised me though, that my father was the one who oversaw all the fundraising and company events, that *he* was the one who had planned them. Thankfully, my dad's right hand man, Rob, didn't seem to mind. One less thing he had to worry about, I guess. He didn't seem particularly interested in the philanthropy division.

I'd thought about that first event, the one on the main street. Where I'd found Cade after he'd left the morning after we...

Then again, when he'd pitched the numbers and the information to my father in that boardroom, how he'd been so compelling that my father greenlit the next two events.

Honestly, I couldn't stop thinking about Cade, period.

His eyes as he held my hand, as he promised me everything would be okay.

No one in my life had ever shown me the genuine kindness that Cade did. Most of the people in my life were nice enough, but it was all polite veneer. When push came to shove, aside from Jamie, I didn't have many people I felt I could actually turn to, to talk to. Who could help me sort my shit out. Who'd hold my hand and tell me it would be okay.

When Cade had asked me on the phone what I needed, I didn't even have to think. I said, "You."

And it was absolutely, one hundred percent true.

"Thanks for your help today, Weston," Cynthia said with a smile as I readied to exit the building.

It was damn nearing five o'clock.

How had the day gone by so quickly?

I nodded in return as I texted Cade.

Just finishing up at the office. Pick you up in ten?

"Of course, if there's anything else I can do, just let me know. I'll probably stop by tomorrow to make sure everything is good for the fundraiser," I said as my phone buzzed nearly instantly with a response.

Sounds good.

"I will let you know if there is anything. Have a good night." Cynthia nodded as I headed out the door, toward home.

CHAPTER THIRTY-SEVEN

Weston

WITH MY PARENTS gone for the time being, the house felt eerily silent. Though I'd always had the option of using one of my dad's cars while in town, I usually didn't like to. Mostly because he was a bit anal and fussy about his babies, more so than he was about his human son.

But something in me was shifting. I could feel it.

I didn't want to share a car with Cade and some random stranger. I wanted him all to myself.

Okay and maybe I wanted to impress him a little. Show him a good time like he'd done with me.

So I grabbed the keys from the carport in the garage for the Audi, which was technically *my* car. I'd just never come back to claim it after I left all those years ago.

When I rejected everything my father offered me because I didn't know if I could be who he wanted me to be. I guess I didn't know who I wanted to be then, either, and in so many ways I still didn't know who I was.

But as I got in the car, hearing that sweet, sexy purr of the engine, I felt at peace. Maybe I didn't have to be someone my father wanted.

Maybe, just maybe being myself was enough.

It certainly seemed enough for Cade.

I pulled out of the garage in search of my prince charming once more, ready to show him the best of both worlds.

Mine, and his.

Because at the end of the day, after a long and arduous day scheduling and approving, and planning this weekend's fundraiser, all I wanted was two things: a stiff glass off Oban, and the man of my fucking dreams.

CHAPTER THIRTY-EIGHT

Weston

"WHEN YOU SAID date, I have to say I didn't expect... this," Cade said with a smirk as he got out of the car.

He'd been pleasantly surprised when I pulled up, even joking with me that he thought maybe I didn't know how to drive since I was chauffeured everywhere.

I assured him I was an excellent driver, and he only shook his head. There were many things I preferred, but more or less it was because I was just accustomed to those things from the life I'd been living.

Not to mention, the men in my life prior to Cade only responded to the overzealous displays of affection like chauffeured rides to and from the hottest clubs, where we'd be seen throwing around the luxuries that built my life.

But that wasn't who I was, not really. I'd done a damn good job of pretending to be the man they all wanted me to be, so much so that I'd convinced myself that was who I was.

But as I exited the car, smiling from ear to ear as the neon glow of M's Place's sign flickered, for the first time I felt free to just... be.

Myself.

I reached for Cade's hand, tugging him closer and he blushed from the movement, but I didn't miss the smile on his face.

"The last time I was here, I had a blast. Met this amazing man who showed me the time of my life," I purred as I pulled him against me, against the hood of the car.

Cade looked up at me from under his lashes, smirking. "Is that so?" he asked coyly.

I nodded as I settled my arms around his hips, holding him close, if only because I didn't want to let him go. Ever. I looked down into his eyes, and my heart skipped a beat.

"And I have it on good authority that it's trivia night. Specifically, Star Wars trivia night," I said with a grin.

Cade's eyes lit up with surprise. "You're serious."

"Dead serious. I thought you might like it."

Cade leaned down, taking my lips like a thief in the night.

"I love it, thank you," he said, his voice barely a whisper.

I melted against his kiss, momentarily debating if I should just scrap this idea altogether, and whisk him away from here, take him back to the Rhodes Family home and shower him with all the love he deserved.

But that could wait.

"Don't thank me yet. Not until we've beaten the other teams," I said as I nipped at his lips, causing a soft chuckle to escape his throat.

"Ah, so there it is. You just want to win cool prizes."

I seriously gazed back at him, my heart in my throat. The need to say it, those three little words was almost overwhelming. But I couldn't. They disappeared on my tongue, making my entire body acutely aware that once I did say them... I'd be crossing a threshold into the unknown.

I'd never told any of the people I'd been with, that I loved them.

Love wasn't what they wanted from me, anyway.

I reached up, brushing some soft, golden locks behind his ear, settling my hand at the base of his neck, fingertips stroking his skin and hair.

"I've already got my prize. The rest is just gravy," I said, my voice betraying no hint at how utterly terrified I was.

I was more exposed in that moment than I'd ever been before, and I watched Cade's entire body relax, felt as he melted into me like butter on a hot griddle.

"Oh, Wes," he breathed, before kissing me again, that explorative tongue of his eliciting a thousand emotions and thoughts from me.

I broke away, nodding toward the entrance.

"Lead the way, Jedi," I said teasingly.

Cade grinned wildly, grabbing my hand and pulling me toward the raucous, music-filled space, and I was happy to follow him.

CHAPTER THIRTY-NINE

Weston

AFTER WINNING THE trivia competition, we were both on cloud nine.

I parked my car outside Cade's house, exiting to open his door and walk him up the sidewalk like a total gentlemen.

He blushed at the notion, taking my arm while using his free one to carry the Han Solo in carbonite statue he'd won as a symbol of power amidst the nerds and fans who'd shown up at the event.

Some I recognized, like the photographer who seemed to be practically everywhere in this town. I'm sure he got a picture of Cade and I with the statue, smiling ear to ear.

I stopped just in front of his door, the air suddenly thickening between us.

"I had an amazing time tonight, Wes," Cade said, setting down his statue on the little metal table beside the door, turning to me as he reached in his pocket for his house keys with his now free hand.

Something about that moment felt different. I watched as he fumbled with his keys, licking his lips.

His breathing increased slightly, as if he was... nervous.

A part of me felt vindicated, validated on a whole other level when Cade got the least bit flustered around me. It was endearing, cute, and made me feel on top of the word.

I loved the effect I had on him, but more so I loved the effect he had on me.

How just being around him made me feel at ease, like I could just... be.

Content, happy.

"Every day I spend with you is amazing," I said honestly, feeling the weight of the unspoken words hiding behind the ones I breathed into life.

Cade sighed as he turned to set his key in the door. He paused after I heard the click.

I'd meant to lean forward and quickly kiss him, tell him goodnight, and thank him for everything. It was late, nearing eleven thirty, and I had intended to be back at the office bright and early when it opened, if only to make sure everything was good to go for the fundraiser, and of course, make sure everything else was operating okay in my father's absence.

But something else happened.

I leaned down and pulled him into my arms, and I whispered, "The fundraiser isn't cancelled anymore."

Cade sank into my hold, a sigh of content leaving his chest.

"It's not?" he asked breathlessly, but the words felt heavy. Like he wanted to say something else, but thought better of it.

I shook my head. "I made sure everything went through. I took care of it myself," I said, feeling the heat between us.

Cade's fingertips grazed over my jaw as he kissed me, and suddenly it was like we had both become someone else entirely. Cade's lips moved slowly against my own, his probing tongue soft and smooth as he slid his fingers in my hair.

Our lips danced together, waltzing down a dark corridor as he spoke.

"I don't want you to go," he whispered against my lips.

His words echoed warnings in my brain, because I knew then that this, this was *it*.

I could have easily kissed him, told him duty called, and I'd see him again over the weekend for the fundraiser.

But I didn't want to go anywhere where Cade wasn't.

I wanted to stay.

With him, in his arms, his heart.

"Then I won't go," I whispered as I wrapped my arms around his waist, tugging him against me with more force than I probably meant to, and it was like a switch was flipped.

Cade turned us around as he fumbled for the door, and we both practically fell in the house. He slammed it shut, never letting up as he continued to kiss me, as his hands slid up and down my back, over my hips, my ass.

I traced my hands over his hips and found the edge of his shirt, pulling at it. Cade met my fervor as he pulled it off, showcasing his perfect toned chest, bathed in the amber light of his foyer.

I dropped the shirt over the arm of the couch, remembering the last time I'd been here. Where I'd watched his eyes fall shut as he came with ecstasy, my name on his tongue like a damn prayer.

He hurriedly popped the buttons on my shirt, and I shrugged out of it as fast as I could, his hands moving to my waistband, pulling me toward him, leading me through the darkened hallway by the kitchen.

The kitchen where I'd realized I was a goner.

Where I'd realized I was in love with him.

I turned us around, slamming his back against the hallway wall. He let out a breathy moan, as I palmed his erection through his jeans, feeling the heat of his chest against my own.

"Fuck, Wes..." he moaned, and I grinned wickedly.

I loved how he said my name.

I loved how his eyes squinted a little bit, how his pouty lips swelled after he'd been kissing me or sucking my cock.

Fuck, I loved his damn risotto and his

ability to make me feel like I was on cloud nine every time he looked at me.

I loved this man, and I intended to make it known even if I couldn't say it out loud.

"You can tell me to stop," I said, giving him an out in case he needed it. I never wanted to assume anything with Cade. I wanted his complete and total consent, as well as his obedience.

He shook his head, grabbing my face in his hands.

"Don't stop," he said, his eyes glazing over.

"Your wish is my command," I said as I worked at his belt.

Cade returned the favor with hurried motion, spinning us around until my back was against the wall, until we were both completely and utterly naked, our bodies melding with the shadows in the hallway.

My cock sprang free, and Cade groaned as I ground myself against him. His hardness against my own was intoxicating. He pulled me back into a dark lit room, his lips seeking mine hurriedly before trailing off over my jaw, my neck. His hands slid up my neck and gripped my hair at the base tightly. The force was sudden, but not unwanted.

"Tell me what you want, Cade," I breathed, my cock aching as he ran his thumb over my sensitive, swollen head.

His lips found their way back to mine, and he pushed me back against something hard, making my knees buckle. I fell back onto a soft, cold cushion, rumpling blankets and sheets.

Cade straddled my legs, nudging them apart as he came up for air, his pupils dilated and full of so much love, so much heat I thought for sure I must have been dreaming.

"You, Wes. I want you," he said, his blue eyes burning into mine.

I slid my hand over his hip, my fingernails digging into his skin as I looked up at him, as he waited for my words.

"Then fucking get on your knees like a good boy and take me," I breathed, watching as his entire body relaxed.

He did as I ordered without question, dropping between my legs and spreading them further apart to make room for him. My cock bounced with anticipation as Cade started at my balls, licking, sucking and massaging them just enough to tease me into oblivion before taking that sweet tongue of his and licking me from base to head, slowly.

It was damn right torture as I thrust my throbbing cock against his lips, seeking entrance. He obliged without words, grabbing me at the base with his hand as he pumped me while simultaneously inching down on my cock.

My legs tightened around his head as pleasure surged through me, as he groaned around me. I could feel the beginnings of my precum forming, and he licked at the saltiness with a hunger that should have damn near been criminal.

My eyes fell shut, and I heard the sound of a drawer, followed by the sound of a cap before I felt a cold wetness spreading around my hole. Instantly, I arched my back off the bed, partly from the temperature but also because I felt the sudden rush of slick, wet fingers teasing my entrance. My ass clenched around the foreign invaders. His thumb brushed the outer skin, massaging me while he moved his fingers in and out slowly, all the while never letting up on my cock.

I thrust my hips into him, the motion driving my cock deeper until I hit the back of his throat, which also pulled his fingers in as far as they could go.

It wasn't enough, I needed more.

I needed...

"Fuck me," I breathed, the words pleading and desperate. I was so close to coming already, I knew I wouldn't be able to last, but I needed to feel something much thicker and bigger than a few fingers right now.

"Please," I added, if only because my manners were ingrained in me.

I wanted to feel him.

I wanted to feel the weight of his body on top of me, the stretch as he filled me, and I wanted to taste myself and my desire on his lips. I wanted to make a mess of him as much as I wanted him to make a mess of me.

I wanted to give Cade the one thing I'd never given anyone else.

Myself.

I'd never let anyone fuck me before. Mostly because in my head it was far more intimate to let someone else possess me like that, to be in control. I'd be at their mercy, instead of the one in control of things, and that was terrifying. In my mind, as stupid as it sounded, I'd always envisioned getting fucked as this ultimate act of love and devotion. It was a whole other thing separate from fast, hard, emotionless sex. In retrospect, I guess I wasn't ready to let anyone in that close, close enough they'd see the masterpiece up front and would have realized it wasn't as beautiful as it looked from afar.

But I had the utmost belief that Cade wouldn't hurt me. That when he looked at me, he saw the mess, and he still thought it was beautiful.

Without a doubt, that's what I wanted. For Cade to *take me*, to look *me* in the eye as he filled me to the brim, to kiss me until I couldn't breathe while he brought me over that threshold into the unknown.

Together.

I trusted him. I knew somehow, though I couldn't explain it, that he'd take care of me and make me feel loved because it was who he was.

And when he looked at me for a moment, my leaking cock rubbing against his abdomen with understanding, I knew that was it.

There was no going back.

"Are you sure?" he asked, his lubricated hand reaching for his own cock, which in the shadowed light looked ominous due to its size and thickness.

I momentarily wondered if he would break me in half, but decided if that was the case, so be it.

I wanted all of Cade Green. I wanted him to ruin me and put me back together again.

"Yeah, I'm sure. If... you're okay with that, I mean," I said, feeling momentarily worried maybe Cade wasn't comfortable being a top, despite his new sudden interest of exploring his confidence, this *new side of him* as he said.

All worry and fear dissipated from his eyes when he looked at me, as he lathered himself up. The wet, slick sounds of the lube as he thrust his cock through his hand was driving me fucking bananas.

I leaned back on the bed, scooting up to give him better access as he slowly, languidly, leaned himself over me. I reached my hand up, fisting in his hair as I whispered against his lips, "I trust you."

He looked at me with vulnerability, his cock poised at my entrance, waiting, teasing me. I thrust myself against him, noting how his cock twitched as I did so.

And when I looked up at him, I knew I was doomed.

Because I was no longer the same man I was before I walked through his door, before I'd set foot in Jasper Springs.

"I love you, Cade." Surprisingly, the words came easily as I whispered them against his lips, kissing him with honesty.

Cade relaxed as I wrapped my leg around his hip, drawing him closer. I wrapped my arms around him, feeling his warmth and skin against my own.

He inched himself inside me slowly, almost torturously slow. Taking his time, acclimating to my tightness, to my warmth, and thanks to the lube on both my ass and his cock, he slid in easily, like silk.

When he bottomed out, I gasped, feeling the fullness of him in every part of me. My spine, my muscles, my heartbeat. For a moment he was still, looking down at me with glassy eyes as his voice shook, his breath heavy.

"I love you too," he said, before he kissed me once more, sliding out of me deliciously slowly, and I felt every inch of him in every part of my body as he reared his hips back. And when he snapped them against me, thrusting hard and deep, I couldn't contain my moan of pleasure or the way my cock throbbed against him. It felt *amazing.*

It didn't even hurt like I thought it would. I felt nothing but pure, blissful pleasure when he fucked me, and emptiness when he slid out of me.

I reached for myself, needing to fuck something, but Cade only swatted my hand away.

"I didn't say you could touch yourself," he said with a wicked gleam, sliding out slowly only to thrust into me with a harder, faster pace, turning me into some desperate, needy bottom.

"Please, sir." I assumed my role almost instantly, gleefully. "I need to come," I moaned against his warm, delicious lips. It wasn't just an act that night. I was practically bursting at the seams, ready to blow.

Cade wrapped his hand around my cock, squeezing and stroking me with the same rhythm as his cock.

I thrust my cock into his hand, my balls tightened and my orgasm was so fucking close. My voice shook, the need and desire thick in the air between us.

"Please, Cade," I moaned in desperation.

Cade's lips shushed me once more, and his rhythm quickened. His slow, deliberate, hard thrusts had gone erratic, and I knew he was close. He fucked me with reckless abandon, with both his hand and his cock until the muscles in my legs and back stiffened and all I knew was the absolute perfection and bliss of this man and all that we were, tangled up together.

His lips coveted my groan as I came, hard and fast in his hand, as he stilled himself, filling me with a warmth I'd never known before. I could feel some of him dripping out of me, down my thigh, and I grabbed his face in my hands, kissing him with praise and love, and everything in between.

"Such a good boy," he whispered softly, breathlessly, in my ear as I clutched his body to mine, absolutely spent before exhaustion took over the both of us.

CHAPTER FORTY

Cade

I WOKE UP to the smelling of burning. Immediately, I jumped out of bed, worrying that something had caught fire. I threw on a pair of boxers quicker than should be humanly possibly, running out to the kitchen only to find Weston, standing there in his black briefs with his perfect ass on display, cooking.

Or more accurately, trying to cook as he jumped away from the bacon pan, cursing.

The sight alone was somehow both endearing and horrific.

I'm going to have to soak that pan for hours...

"Good morning," I said as a grin erupted on my face.

Weston turned, his deep green eyes lighting up the minute he saw me.

"Oh thank God you're up," he said as he went back to the stove.

I watched as he set about to cracking some eggs, fingering out bits of shell, no doubt since he didn't crack them lightly on the side of the pan, and I decided to step in.

He looked a little... out of his element.

But damn it if it wasn't the best way to wake up.

At least I know the house isn't burning down.

"You, uh... need some help here?" I asked as I approached him, reaching out gingerly to pull him away from the stove.

He turned in my grasp, his gaze dipping to my lips.

"That depends on your definition of help," he teased as he nipped my bottom lip, making my stomach flip and the blood rush straight to my cock.

"I mean, your bacon is burning..." I said as I pointed to the sizzling pan that looked encrusted in black char at this point.

Weston pushed me aside, turning the pieces over with a satisfied sound.

"It is not burning. It is char-grilled. It's a gourmet thing."

"Hmmm, so that's what they call it," I teased, but decided to take his lead. Instead of pushing, trying to take over, I took a seat at my island and just... watched.

I just watched the son of a millionaire make me breakfast in his underwear and it was glorious.

Entertaining too, as I watched him bustle about my kitchen like he lived there, opening and shutting cupboards, pouring coffees and orange juices, and trying to set the table like this place was a five star restaurant.

The food itself wasn't terrible... even the char-grilled bacon.

But nothing was as delicious as the man who made it, the man who really did look like he belonged here.

With me.

Just as I finished my last piece of toast, Weston's phone rang.

"Hello?" he answered, looking a bit worried, but instantly relaxed after a moment or two.

I decided to leave him to whoever he spoke to, and instead focused on cleaning up the mess from Weston's cooking extravaganza.

"I'll be right there," he said with a sigh as he hung up.

I turned to look at him. "Everything okay?"

He nodded. "My dad's getting discharged," he said calmly.

"That's a good thing, right?" I asked, immediately heading over to him. I didn't miss how his shoulders tightened, or how his entire body locked up, the tension obviously spreading.

And so I did the only thing I could think of. I pulled Weston into my arms, and I told him it was going to be okay.

He was going to be okay.

He wrapped his arms around me, tightening his hold and nodded, leaning down to brush my lips with a gentle, whisper of a kiss, and he murmured, "I know."

"I've got to get going, but, I'll call you later?" he asked as he moved out of my arms toward the bedroom.

My heart was somehow both so full and so broken as I watched this perfect morning completely disintegrate.

The night before he'd told me he loved me.

I'd said it back because it was the truth, but as I watched him get ready to head out, it dawned on me that we hadn't really talked about what we were, or where this... connection, this love we did have... where it fit into his life.

Weston had come to Jasper Springs on business, but he hadn't agreed to stay indefinitely. In fact, despite his father's insistence he take the reins, Weston had made no move to do so.

Did he plan on heading back to the city where he lived?

Would we just become some long-distance relationship where we caught up on the weekends until it was time for him to fly off somewhere else?

I wasn't sure.

But despite the anxiety, despite the thoughts that threatened to upend this beautiful, perfect morning, I chose to believe that maybe things would work out.

After all, believing in the good things, having hope, that's a hell of a lot more difficult than believing things won't work out in your favor

And sometimes, life does give you exactly what you ask for.

Like a sexy corporate leading man who falls for a small town heartthrob and they live happily ever after.

So as I kissed Weston goodbye, and readied myself for work, I chose to believe in us.

That whatever happened, we'd figure it out. Together. And for the first time in my life, that was enough.

CHAPTER FORTY-ONE

MY DAD LOOKED a thousand times better than he had when I'd visited him after he'd had his heart attack.

My mother also looked a little more put together than she had been in recent days, though I couldn't be certain if that was because she'd had a facial or if she was just happy my father was doing better.

Margo had set to preparing a mid-morning meal, at my mother's request. Though my father kept asking for his chocolate chip muffins, which seemed to have been left off the menu.

"I heard you've been helping out down

at the company in my absence," my father said as he took a sip of his tea. After some begging and pleading, my mother had agreed to leave us alone, though I suspect she was hovering because the doctor had blatantly told us to keep my dad's stress levels down.

I knew it was no secret I added to his stress, and the feeling was mutual, but something about that day felt different.

I felt different.

"Well, I mean you *did* just announce your retirement and dramatically had a heart attack. I don't think the ink was dry on the papers yet, so..."

"Cynthia told me you reinstated the fundraiser. Took over the calls, arranging everything."

"I did," I said, feeling a sense of accomplishment for once.

My dad stared straight on out the window, watching the birds fly to the massive feeder my mother had put in when I was a kid. I used to love sitting in the four-season room, where we were, and watching all the wildlife when I was home in the summer as a kid.

Jasper Springs was so lush and green, full of wildlife, and I guess a charm I never really appreciated.

And sitting there with my dad, I had to admit… it had a calming effect on me, and him.

For once, we weren't at one another's throats.

Perhaps Hell has frozen over.

"Now that I'm out of the hospital, I will need to move on naming my replacement. The ink has likely dried on the papers, as you say."

His words weren't all that different from what I'd heard many times, but this time, I could hear the sadness, the exhaustion in his voice. I stole a look at him, noting his profile as he stared at the birds. While my mother had a constant need to try every face cream and beauty treatment available because she didn't want to "look old" like she felt, my father had let age flourish on him. But as I looked at him that day, I realized that it was not an easy decision for him. Not because I had been so adamant, but because he truly *loved* his job. He loved getting up and going to meetings, and overseeing spreadsheets, and planning fundraisers. He loved coming home to his wife and the life they'd build together, even if it wasn't perfect because he had a pain in the ass son who never visited and argued with him all the time.

"I know I've asked you a million times, and a million times you've told me no. So this will be the last time. If you truly don't want to be a part of this company, I will accept your resignation. You can go home to your condo and live your life how you see fit, and I won't ever ask you again."

His words fell on me and for the first time, I realized I couldn't say no, entirely.

No, I don't want this. No, I don't want to be you.

When the truth of the matter was, the life I had in the city wasn't really the life I wanted at all.

In fact, it was *everything* I had never wanted, and I'd deluded myself into thinking it was mine. That I thrived and loved all the late night club dates, the pretty boys who looked good in the digs I bought them, hanging on my arm for the moment they existed in my life.

But I wasn't happy.

The alcohol always ran out, and the men always disappeared. The condo was always empty, silent, and I was just... existing. I was passing time until the next dopamine rush, until the next argument. Until the next... everything.

But I didn't feel that way in Jasper Springs.

Not anymore.

I realized at that moment, that I could have everything I wanted, if I just fucking jumped. That everything I'd been searching for was right there in Jasper Springs, all along.

"What if..." My voice shook as the reality of the truth ransacked me. "What if I fuck up?" I asked.

My father turned toward me, appraising me with his stoic gaze, his lips pulling up at the corners to show the hint of a smile.

"You think I was perfect, Weston? That I knew what I was doing when I started this company? When I met your mom? When I had you?" He chortled gruffly.

"You'll always make mistakes. You're human. But your heart is in the right place, and you show up and you do your best. That's all you have to do."

"Can I... can I... think about it?" I said, the words making me feel somehow lighter.

My dad smiled, nodding.

"You've got twenty four hours. I won't be back in the office to start the hiring process until tomorrow evening."

"Tomorrow evening is the fundraiser," I said.

"So it is," he responded, taking another sip of his tea. We both sat there, staring at the birds until my tea had gone cold.

CHAPTER FORTY-TWO

Cade

THE JASPER SPRINGS Pet Hospital always closed early on Fridays. With the reinstatement of the last Rhodes Enterprises event, Diane felt it was important that we all attend, not just me.

Though with my track record being pretty decent from the last two events, she wanted me to man the booth, and surprisingly, I'd jumped at the opportunity.

I'd never really liked working with the public, which was one of the reasons I loved working with animals as opposed to humans. But something in me changed over the last week. I still got nervous, sure, but after speaking at two events and in front of some very important people, I knew I could do it.

And when Diane had asked me to be the person to accept the check, the big show of it, anyway, in front of our community, I wholeheartedly agreed.

We'd raised a ton of money from the last two events that I knew would go to great use, and I'd never been more proud of the hospital, or myself.

I waited around backstage for almost an hour until things actually started moving, and Mr. Rhodes came out on stage. I knew from Weston that he'd been doing better since he got home, and had already started to transition his replacement.

Though Weston was pretty tight-lipped about the future of his family's company, and I wasn't going to press him. I knew it was a sore subject, and he'd been through a lot this week. Though I'd garnered it'd been a lot for the last few years, if not his life, even though I had no proof, just from the bits and pieces he did share with me.

I wasn't even surprised to see Weston on stage, standing next to his father, looking every bit Mr. Sexy Suit.

I tried to catch his gaze, but he refused to look my way, instead focusing out over the crowd.

Maybe he doesn't know it's me accepting the check...

His father droned on about his heart attack, the company, and what it meant to him, his family and his community. He spoke about matching *all* of our donations and what we'd raised, and my heart nearly burst.

I hadn't known that much. I knew the events were good, good enough that we'd done three, but Diane had never said anything about Rhodes matching our numbers.

Just as my musings started to spin, his father called my name, loud and clear.

Shit, that's my cue!

I took a deep breath, stilling the nerves that still threatened to rile up in me, being as I was walking out on stage in front of a sea of people. But I didn't focus on them.

I only focused on Weston, who now met my gaze and was smiling with pride.

Someone walked out to hand Weston a large posterboard-sized check, and he took it easily.

I knew it was just a show, but my heart still lifted when I read the numbers, 20,000.

We'd raised more money than I ever thought possible, and Rhodes had matched our efforts. To say I was floored and humbled was an understatement.

Weston handed me my check with a smirk and a wink.

"Such a good boy," he said in a whisper only we could hear, making me turn ten shades of red on stage in front of everyone.

And then he took the microphone from his father to make his own speech.

"Rhodes Enterprises has always been a fixture of this town and community. At the heart of this company, we are built by your compassion, your kindness, and your passion. Which is why events like this one, and the others you may or may not have attended this week are so critical. This company is nothing without its community. It's taken me a long time to understand that, but now that I do, it is my promise as the future CEO of Rhodes Enterprises that there will be more of a focus going forward on this community as a whole. Because you aren't just consumers to us. You're family."

My blood chilled and I swear I almost dropped the damn check.

Weston accepted the job.

That meant...

"I'm sure you will *all* have a lot of questions, but those will need to be saved and addressed for another time. Congratulations to Cade and the Jasper Springs Pet Hospital on raising such an extraordinary amount. No doubt this will help so many animals and the humans who care for them. Well done!" he said as he clapped, and the audience roared with applause in return.

Someone came out and grabbed the check, I think it was Diane. Weston ushered me off the stage into the wings.

I felt frozen, immobilized.

What just fucking happened?

"You're..."

"Staying," Weston said as soon as we'd gotten off the stage.

They words hit me like a thousand sacks of potatoes.

He was staying.

Here, in Jasper Springs.

"Why?" I asked, suddenly overcome

with too much emotion I could barely process his words.

Weston reached out to brush my hair behind my ear, his eyes sparkling in the light.

"Because everything I've ever wanted is here, and I'd be a fool to give it all up."

"Everything?" I asked, my voice shaking.

Weston settled his free hand on my hip and pulled me close, his lips brushing mine softly.

"Everything," he whispered before he kissed me, and I melted into his arms like butter.

Sometimes things work out.

And when they do... it's the most amazing thing in the world.

"You want to get out of here?" Weston asked haughtily.

"Yeah, I think I do," I answered confidently, my smile stretching ear to ear.

"I think I know just the place."

EPILOGUE

Cade

"I WOULD LIKE to propose a toast to my matchmaking skills," Dawson said as he raised his beer glass.
I swatted at him, causing him to move and slosh some beer over the sides.

"Dawson, stop," I pleaded.

"No, no, it's fine. Let the man have his moment," Weston said with a wink.

"Thank you, Weston. Or should I call you *Mr. Rhodes*?" Dawson taunted him.

Well, it's better than a derogatory nickname...

"You can call me whatever you want, Mr. March," Weston said as he took a sip of his Oban.

"Smart man. As I was saying, a toast to my matchmaking skills. It was in this very bar that I *shoved* you two together. So, I'd like everyone to remember that when you two get married."

My cheeks flushed instantly. It wasn't like I hadn't thought about the idea, but even I knew things were still way too new and fresh, but the fact Weston didn't even balk at the mention made my heart flutter like a flock of seagulls.

"Mhmmm. Shame your skills don't carry over into your own life... or is that just because Mr. March has a tiny firehose?"

"Fuck you, Mitch. Ya'll know this *firehose* is a damn triumph."

"Funny, I don't see anyone around here limping from your *triumph.*"

Weston let out a raucous roar of laughter as I shook my head.

"Fuck, Nolan's here," Dawson said, his voice shifting from fun and relaxed to angry and annoyed.

We all turned in the direction of his gaze to see a medium height man who looked like something out of Revenge of the Nerds. White button down with pens on the pocket, khaki pants, and glasses.

"Is that the claims adjuster who's always making your life miserable?" I asked, taking in the sight of Dawson's nemesis.

Nolan Harding had a knack for showing up at almost every fire Dawson and the firehouse showed up at. He was always going over every report with a fine-toothed comb, which pissed Dawson off.

I'd heard more rants about Nolan Harding than anyone should be subjected to, and I had to admit, seeing him in the flesh in all his nerdy attire was actually comical.

This was the guy Dawson hated?

He's like Harry Potter.

Dawson's lips pulled into a tight line.

"Hold my beer. I'm about to go make *his* life a living hell for once."

Mitch rolled his eyes.

"Remember, ladies don't start fights..." he taunted Dawson as he got up.

"No, but they fucking finish them," Dawson said in a chipper tone, leaving us to ourselves.

"Did you really date him?" Weston asked, raising an eyebrow.

I thought he would have been pissed when Dawson essentially dropped the tidbit earlier, after I'd officially introduced him to my friends as my actual boyfriend.

"Yeah, but obviously I regained my smarts."

Weston grinned.

"So, the firehose…"

"Not bad, but you're a thousand times better," I said, flashing him with a wicked grin.

"You are a smart man," Weston said as he took a sip.

Mitchell got up.

"All right, well, it's karaoke night, so I'm not sitting around here while you two get all cute and handsy and Dawson's off fucking shit up. I'm singing."

I nodded in response.

"We'll be up there sooner or later," Weston said confidently.

"Oh, we will?" I asked, raising an eyebrow, challenging him.

"Absolutely. But I believe it's my turn to pick the song," he said as he pulled me between his legs, wrapping his arms around me.

The scent of scotch on his breath mixed with his cologne was heady and made me breathless.

"Fine. But you're going to owe me

later," I said, kissing him back.

"A very smart man once told me I make up very well."

His hands slid up and down my back, his gaze holding me in place. It was like the rest of the world fell away, like there was only us.

And I knew it would always be like that.

"I'll hold you to that," I said as I wrapped my arms around his neck, and kissed him like they do in the movies, our lips, tongues, and hearts singing happily ever after in the story of our own making.

Thank you for reading Cade and Weston's story.

If you enjoyed this book, please return to your favorite retailer and leave a review. Even a few words could mean the world to an author.

Continue the series with Dawson's story, Book 2 in Jasper Springs!

OTHER BOOKS BY EVIE

Federal Protection Agency
Mason
Rafe
Ryzen
Cooper
Noah
Damien
Sebastian
Gabe
Logan

Ruthless Empire
Courting Danger
Chasing Danger
Kissing Danger

Smokejumpers
Hawke
Cyrus
Jase
Gage
Jackson
Xavier

Jasper Springs
Cade
Dawson
Drew
Grayson
Riley
Mitch

From The Edge
Shattered
Runaway
Jaded
Rescue
Hidden
Tormented

Gray Vale Pack
His Fated Mate
His Wounded Warrior
His Healing Heart

ABOUT THE AUTHOR

Evie Riley is a prolific, neurodivergent author known for her captivating MM romance novels. She has gained a significant following and topped the LGBT+ action and adventure bestseller charts with her series.

Evie's writing style often explores dark and gritty themes where her men must overcome difficult obstacles in their search for love, but she has also ventured into sweeter small-town romances, incorporating tropes like enemies-to-lovers, friends-to-lovers, age-gap, and forced proximity. She is known for crafting engaging romantic suspense novels and has a knack for creating interconnected series worlds that keep readers invested.

Interestingly, Ms. Riley has hinted at exploring new genres, such as Alien Omegaverse Romance, in the future.

Outside of writing, she enjoys spending time at the beach and has a quirky personality, described by her partner as ranging from cute to deadly, depending on her blood-chocolate levels.

Evie spends her nights writing bad boys in love, and her days wrangling the sweet boys she loves.